I0623490

Talismans and Turmoil

Astoria Wright

Faerie Apothecary Mysteries
Book 6

Talismans and Turmoil

Published by Novelwright Press, LLC
novelwright.com

Cover Art by Viyiwi
etsy.com/shop/beatriceviyiwi

Edited by 529Books
529books.com

Table of Contents

Map of Moss Hill

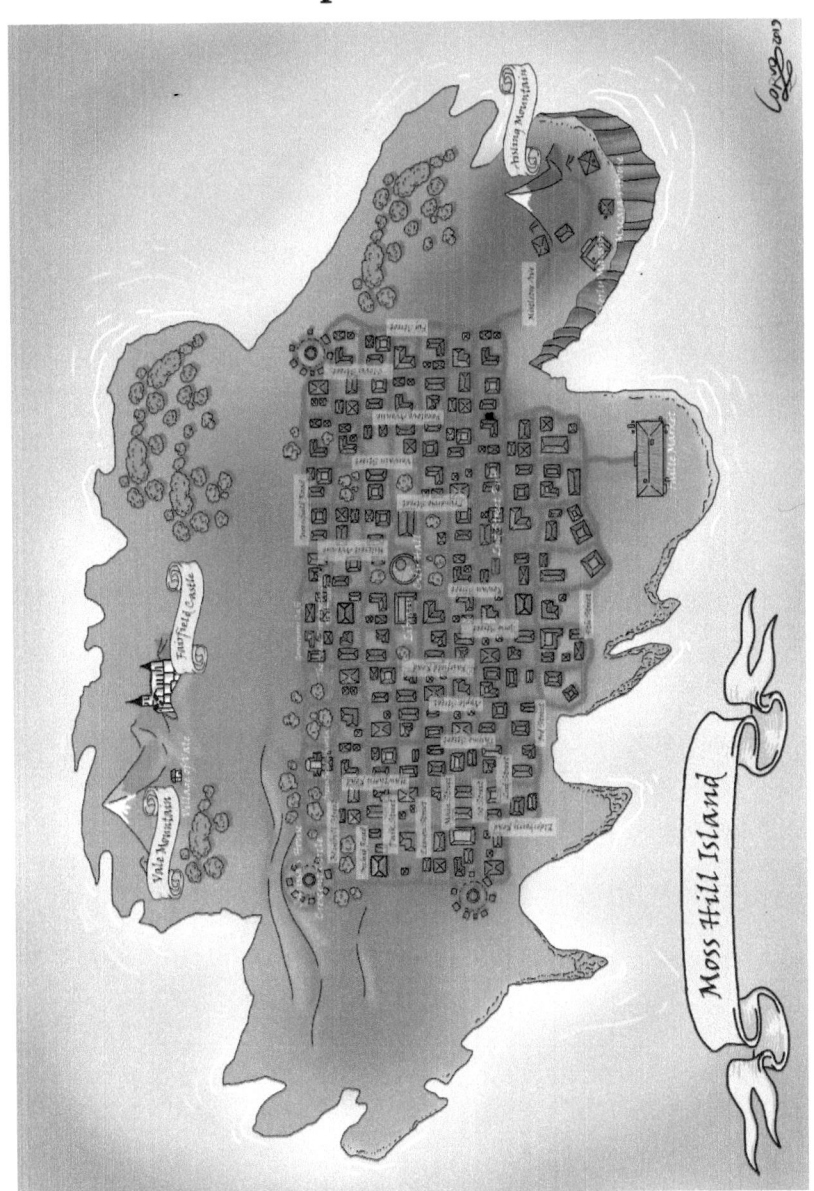

Chapter 1

A Maiden Voyage

The Second Street Pub accommodated poetry reads, improv groups, and small-town bands, and tonight the crew of the *Scuabtuinne*. The red booths and the fire blazing in the brick oven gave the place warmth, though at least one table was feeling the chill from the fall weather blowing in off the sea. Carissa Shae and her fiancé, Cameron Larke, had differing opinions about leaving tomorrow on the legendary ship for an adventure that would determine the fate of their cozy island town of Moss Hill. They also differed on their opinions of the famous captain of the *Scuabtuinne*, Logan, whose bellowing out sea ballads had sent Nan home early with a headache. Carissa found herself coming down with the same condition.

Cameron didn't seem to mind. "He's got a good singing voice, and so do his druid crewmen. Can't you just enjoy his songs and stories for one night?"

Maren Raines, Carissa's assistant and best friend, wasn't having it. She tossed her brownish-blonde hair behind her ears and stood. "I have half a mind to have them thrown out."

"Or ask your boyfriend to ban them from the island altogether, dear," Holly said in her motherly voice. "And I'll be glad to help." Though only a stout, three-foot-tall bean tighe, Holly was a fearsome sight when angry.

"Now, now," said Carissa's leprechaun tailor and neighbor, Barnaby. The barstool gave Barnaby enough height to take hold of Maren's sleeve. He was fast enough to catch Holly's arm, too, before she jumped down to follow her human friend's folly. "They're just having fun, and the town's enjoying it, so let it be."

The town *was* enjoying it. Practically everyone Maren had invited had gathered clear across the pub to hear the captain regaling tales of maritime adventures, which left Holly, Barnaby, and Maren alone to pay any mind to the guests of honor.

"It's fine, Maren," Carissa said. "Honestly, I don't mind the stories—it's the hubris behind them."

"He's well accomplished and proud of it." Cameron shrugged.

Carissa said, "True enough. I'm glad to know that we'll be in good hands out there, anyway."

"I enjoyed the stories," Barnaby said, adding under his breath, "for the first three hours."

"I could do without the loud sea-shanties." Holly cradled her ears for emphasis.

"Just one night," Maren snorted, repeating Cameron's words as if he'd been joking. "What if he does this every night?"

Carissa's green eyes met Cameron's brown with the same panic. He snapped out of it first, reaching to take her hands in his. His soothing tone calmed her nerves.

"I'm sure he'll have plenty to do with a whole magical ship to manage."

"The *Scuabtuinne*," Barnaby whistled. "Never thought I'd see it in your lifetime." He tipped his glass in Cameron's direction.

This time Cameron shared a glance with Maren. Carissa couldn't share in that reaction. Barnaby's reference to their human lifespans would not apply to her as a half-elf. *Half-elf, part human, and part Tuatha de Danann*, she had to remind herself.

All those years she'd spent thinking she was half-human and half-elf without a hint of her grandfather being part of the ancient faerie race seemed wasted. Now that she was going to confront the Tuatha de Danann on their mythical island, she couldn't help but think she ought to have trained from a young age to meet them.

Like Logan.

If the stories he'd told all night were true, he was a formidable Tuatha de Danann in his own right, having saved many a lost ship and fought many a pirate in his immortal life. Little Timmy Harbridge, now nine and full of curiosity, asked Logan a variety of questions as Carissa watched them from across the pub, to which Logan laughed wholeheartedly and answered every one. Timmy's eyes lit up with all the wonder of a child listening to his hero. Good for him. Good for Logan.

But it was terrible for Carissa that she felt so unprepared next to this conquering hero. Her father hadn't properly taught her about her elf-light magic, and her mother hadn't even mentioned she was half-Tuatha de Danann, much less trained her in the most powerful fae magic in the world.

Did she even want that kind of magic? She didn't want to go on this journey, let alone to be Tuatha de Danann. She just wanted a simple life, on this little island of human and fae neighbors, running an apothecary shop on the corner of Greenfield and Gorse Streets.

A gust of wind came in through the door as a customer left. The autumn breeze filled the pub and tousled her auburn hair. The view through the windows was dark. Squeezing Cameron's hands with her fingers, Carissa said, "I think it's time I get home."

Cameron leaned in for a kiss. "You're sure you don't want me to drive you?" he asked when they'd pulled away.

"No, I'd like one last look at the island." Cameron kept hold of her fingertips. She smiled reassuringly, running a hand through his chestnut-brown hair. "I'll be fine."

Maren rolled her eyes. "You act like you're never coming back to Moss Hill. You know you promised you'd only be gone a week."

"No, *you* insisted I could only be gone a week. Macara said it could take longer. It certainly would with a human-made ship." Carissa's chiding went unheard, as evidenced by Maren sipping away at her drink, no longer looking at her. Carissa grabbed her purse and looked at Holly.

"Don't look at me, dear. I've as much control over your friend as I have on Macara, which is to say none. Of course, anyone with half a brain wouldn't dare challenge a Tuatha de Danann—much less two." She winked at Carissa, knowing full well that not everyone in the pub knew Carissa's true nature. Every islander was aware that Macara was a Tuatha de Danann, but many also felt she was to blame for the recent troubles in Moss Hill.

Macara meant well, though, and so did Holly, so Carissa smiled. The grin became a laugh as Maren's arms wrapped around her like a boa constrictor.

"I'm just going to miss you so much!" Maren said.

Barnaby helped pry her away from a reddening Carissa. "No tears now, you still have both of us, love."

"And your boyfriend, dear," Holly added.

"Yeah," Cameron said, looking around. "Speaking of which, why isn't Reginald here? I know you said he'd be late, but three hours? Government business doesn't take that long—not on this island."

Not unless there was a fae-related emergency, Carissa knew Cameron was thinking. He was no longer interim mayor, no longer even working for the city council, but he still looked toward the pub door with that worried grimace. Inevitably, his hand found the back of his neck, where it always went to soothe his nerves. Carissa placed a hand atop it.

"I'm sure everything's fine," she said.

Maren shrugged. "You know Reg, he gets an idea and is lost in it for hours. I think his true love is actually Moss Hill."

"Jealous, dear?" Holly asked.

"If Moss Hill were a woman. Nah, I'm fine with him obsessing about books over blondes and brunettes." She reached for her phone. "I'll send him a message anyway."

Carissa drew in one last deep breath, taking in the red brick walls, the giant clock above the bar, the wooden tables, and the sounds of the mixed Mossie accents. The only place on earth humans and fae came together—this is what she was sailing overseas to protect.

The Tuatha de Danann would have to break their non-interference rule to help Moss Hill fend off the unseelie. Reginald Smith, Maren's boyfriend and current mayor of Moss Hill, had gone months ago to plead the case for helping the town. This had bought them some time. But unless Carissa presented a peaceful plan for uniting the fae people with humanity, the experiment of Moss Hill would end, and the Tuatha de Danann would seal off the human world from the Otherworld of the fae forever, just as they had planned before Moss Hill's creation.

Any fae who managed to stay on the human side of the barrier would be free to use their powers unchecked against humanity. There were not enough humans with magic, or druids, on earth to protect them. The unseelie, evil faeries, would have total rule over the human world. What's more, Moss Hill's vision of fae and human neighbors coexisting peacefully around the globe would be forever lost.

Carissa pictured the pub under unseelie rule: with humans serving the fae. Unseelie faeries taunting them, using misguided magic. She shuddered at the thought. The Mossies could not lose to evil faeries.

She had to leave, not just the island, but Carissa had to leave the pub right now if she was going to sleep at all tonight. Her eyes scanned the tables and booths until she spotted a group of three-inch nature faeries laughing at one of Logan's latest jokes.

She smirked. Of course, they'd want to be in on the action. A Tuatha de Danann captain was too big a deal for them to resist. They'd nestled onto the round table right next to Logan's arm.

He pounded a fist to emphasize a point in his story, and they jumped. Their eyes locked on to him even as they settled back onto the table. Their hands on their chins made them look like lovesick schoolgirls in their purple flower petal dresses. Not just Chaos and Cynth—even Cynth's brother, Hiya, in the boyish suit Barnaby had made him from a yellow hyacinth flower, was practically drooling.

"So there I stood," Logan's voice softened with suspense, "outside the tallest gates of the grandest castle atop the most massive mountain any eyes had ever seen. I struck the doors again with my fists and demanded entry, but still they would not let me in.

"'What are your skills?' they asked. 'What can you offer the Tuatha de Danann that we do not have already?'

"'I am a blacksmith,' I said.

"'We have one,' they answered.

"'I am a warrior,' I said.

"'We have many,' they replied.

"'I am a strategist,' I said. "But, again, they had one skilled in the art of war, so they reiterated that they had no need for me. Each thing I listed was bantered: swordsman, harpist, poet, historian, druid, craftsman—even a hero to my people—and yet they still would not let me in."

"What did you do?" Timmy asked.

"Hush, let him tell us," his mother chided.

Logan smiled, clearly relishing the anticipation in their eyes. He leaned in. "I asked them if they had a single person with all those skills, and if they did, I said I'd gladly challenge them at any task they set before me."

"Did you—"

"Hush, Timmy!"

Logan smiled wider at the mother-child interaction until he laughed. "They did not have a single person with all those skills, so they had to let me in!"

Every Mossie and crewmate laughed and remarked to one another about Logan's cleverness and bravery. Carissa, standing unnoticed in the back, couldn't help but ask a question amid all the mirth.

"But aren't you Tuatha de Danann? Why did you have to ask to be let in?"

Logan's smile tempered itself with wistful memory. "A half-Tuatha de Danann and half-Fomorian was not welcome at the time. The two were enemies."

"Are they still? Enemies, I mean," Timmy asked.

"My boy, there are no more Fomorians in all the world." His voice quieted to just above a whisper, "There are no enemies to the Tuatha de Danann anymore."

Carissa felt a chill rush down her spine. Logan recovered quickly, starting up a song like the loss of his people was nothing—or nothing on which to linger.

"Chaos, Hiya, Cynth, let's go," Carissa called.

The nature faeries frowned but did not argue. It was past their bedtime, except for Chaos, whose curfew Carissa could never set. Chaos never followed rules or orders, but she did like to be a part of giving them. She shot faerie dust behind Hiya and Cynth to make them go faster. They quibbled with fists but flew ahead anyway, landing snugly on Carissa's shoulders.

Chaos took the top of her forehead, pulling as if she were a horse. Carissa snatched her and placed her safely in her purse. Chaos leaned over the open zipper, staring disapprovingly at Carissa. If Chaos were anything but tired, she would have zipped right out of that purse.

Carissa opened the pub door and went out into the night. "No antics. We go straight home and right to bed. We've got to be up early tomorrow."

Hiya and Cynth shifted their weights on her shoulders as if they'd just sat up straight. Carissa hated to let them down, but she had to stop them from getting their hopes up. She held up a finger.

"No, not the two of you. We already talked about this. You two are staying in Moss Hill. You've got to keep the other nature faeries' spirits up. Summer is here, and you know how the garden needs to be kept in order."

The faeries sunk down as she continued her list of excuses as to why they couldn't go on an epic sailing adventure. She knew they could tell she was lying, but one lies to keep one's friends safe. She knew they'd understand that, too.

Chaos had more magic than them and had already traveled by sea. All alone, in fact. She would be a help on the voyage. Besides, she wouldn't take no for an answer.

Carissa continued spouting off pretend reasons for Hiya and Cynth to stay home when a hand grabbed her out of nowhere. A sick feeling churned in the pit of her stomach, and she found herself snatching the hand to steady herself.

The scenery changed from the road where her blue beach-cruiser sat to a fireplace with a flickering hearth. Hiya and Cynth flew to the air in front of her, taking on ridiculous fighting stances. Chaos disappeared from sight, but Carissa didn't panic. The scent of a garlic potato soup bubbling tickled her nose. Her stomach calmed, and she breathed a sigh of relief. A quaint rooster sculpture on a rustic kitchen counter told her she was safe even before she saw her captors.

"Alden, Macara," Carissa looked at the two to her right, a dark haired man sulking by the fire, and an attractive brunette sitting in a queenly posture on a floral sofa chair, "why couldn't you just come to the pub if you wanted to speak?"

"Because," a voice startled her from behind. A woman with long black hair, dark eyes, and a cheery nature faerie on her shoulder, approached from the living room window to the couch. Carissa descended into the cushions. A surprise was a surprise but seeing Macara's eccentric sister, Raven, in human business attire was a shock to Carissa's system.

Raven finished her thought: "There are things to discuss that are not for human or fae ears."

Carissa's lips thinned, never mind the nature faeries settling themselves on the sofa, the Mossies in the pub wouldn't have been listening to Raven today anyway. They were too busy with Logan. Still, Raven might have a point. She'd set up the whole sea-faring mission after all.

"You won't be going on this mission alone," Macara said.

"I know, Cam is coming with me," Carissa assured.

"We don't mean any humans. You'll need some fae support as well."

"Logan is—"

"Logan is not fae…and he's not who we mean," Raven said.

Carissa bit her lip. She knew what Raven meant. He was Tuatha de Danann, so not fae. Raven had told her once that for humans and fae to be allowed to continue living together on the island, a human, fae, and Tuatha de Danann would have to agree that the experiment of Moss Hill had been a success. The agreement had to be sealed in blood and magic before the Tuatha de Danann Council. Then and only then, might the Tuatha de Danann agree to help protect the Mossies from unseelie attacks.

But Carissa had thought that Raven had meant her— that with all three types of blood, she had enough magic to complete the agreement herself. Of course, agreements were rarely with only one person, so Carissa couldn't be surprised if another person was needed.

"Who's going with me?"

Alden turned from the mantle to face Raven and Carissa.

"Alden?" Carissa asked. She'd be glad for his company, but barring the fact that he was needed in Moss Hill, he didn't seem to be the best candidate. "But he's the ankou—I'm sorry,

Alden, but I don't think that's, strictly speaking, fae, is it? If you need a fae for the agreement—"

She looked at Raven, who was shaking her head. "Not Alden. It's not an agreement, it's a binding, and I've already told you your powers alone are needed for that. I'm sending a fae only because this particular faerie is nearly as powerful as the sidhe elders and quite possibly as impressive with magic as Jane is with her druidess powers. Since we can't send Jane with you, we're sending the next best person for your protection."

It made sense. Raven and Macara couldn't send Jane with her because Moss Hill needed protection. Macara was staying, and Raven was doing something she didn't care to explain to Carissa, but both were not technically supposed to interfere. They were still bound by Tuatha de Danann rules, even though they did bend them.

But the mission was supposed to be secret. They hadn't shared the real purpose of their mission with any Mossie. Even Maren thought they were going to Scotland to seek advice from the headmaster of a school for druid warriors.

"Why do I need protection? You said the unseelie wouldn't dare attack the *Scuabtuinne*. And I've been training my Tuatha de Danann powers, and Logan is—"

"Carissa," Alden said, "can't you just take the help? I—*we*—will feel better if you're protected."

Carissa fell silent. She'd never heard Alden speak with such force. Carissa almost chided him for the tone he used—as if this was not a voyage for fair maidens who became damsels in distress. She fought the impulse to remind him that she was as powerful as she was unpracticed at magic. Though the last part of her thought made it a fair point that she might need protection after all. Carissa accepted the help with a nod.

"Good," Raven said. "We'll send her to the docks at sunrise."

"Her?" Carissa inquired.

"Tabitha." Macara's smile was priceless.

Carissa's mouth hung open. Hiya and Cynth rolled with laughter. Even Chaos held back a chuckle as she waved a finger at her fellow nature faeries to tell them to stop. Carissa could imagine the hours of nonstop talking, the frivolous magic spells, the ridiculous foods Tabitha made that Carissa always ate just to be polite.... It was too late. She'd already accepted the help.

But at what cost?

Chapter 2

Stowaway Fae

A knocking at her front door awoke Carissa at sunrise. Chaos, whose chocolate cosmos plant had taken permanent residence on the windowsill overlooking the garden, tugged her kerchief-blanket up over her head and rolled toward the chocolate scented flowers. Carissa tossed her own blankets aside and willed herself up out of bed and down the steps to where she could already hear footsteps in the hall. Eyes still fuzzy from sleeping, Carissa blinked until the image of Nan became clear. Tying her robe as she walked, Nan complained.

"Who in the world would wake the neighborhood at five in the morning?"

The question and another round of door-knocking set Carissa's elf-ears tingling. At this hour, all she could think was that someone was in trouble. And if they were coming to her, they either needed her help as an apothecary or as a fae. Or there was some kind of library emergency for Nan, but that seemed unlikely.

Carissa flicked the outdoor light on and opened the bright red door. Outside, a tall figure in a freshly pressed brown suit fiddled nervously with a hat. Slender pointed ears and a wiry frame reminded her of Fudge, Jane Everly's butler, but as he met her eyes with a smile, Carissa recognized him as a different elfkin.

"Sal? What are you doing here?" She opened the door wider, vaguely aware that her baggy red- and white-striped pajamas made her look like a kid on Christmas, but they were the only ones she hadn't packed. Sal, on the other hand, looked like he was dressed for church, though he had never attended. She'd never seen him so fashionable.

"I'm so sorry to be a bother, Cari, but I thought it best to catch you before you get to the boat."

"Is everything all right?" Carissa asked.

"All's fine, only Miss Hela—"

"Is it the baby?" Nan wedged herself between Carissa and the doorway. Up until recent months, Sal's employer had been the head elf, Rolin of Vale. But since his daughter's marriage and pregnancy, Rolin had reassigned him to Hela's household. Since he had practically helped in raising Hela, he didn't seem to mind.

"No, nothing like that. But she did send me for some herbs."

"Well, Sal, Maren could help you with that when the shop opens."

"Actually, Hela insisted that I get them from you before you leave on your trip."

"Oh, that girl," Nan said. "Come into the kitchen and I'll fix you a nice cup of tea. You best get ready, Cari."

No matter how much she liked Sal, Carissa did not need this today. She trudged upstairs, fighting her desire to crawl back under the covers, and reached for the clothes she'd set atop her luggage for this morning.

Chaos rolled to face the dresser. One tiny eyelid raised and shut. Carissa dressed, combed her hair, and made her bed all while the gentle chime of Chaos's pretend snoring filled the air beside the window.

"I know you're awake." Carissa lifted the handkerchief from Chaos, who curled into a ball. Carissa wouldn't let her off the hook that easily. "You would've had to get up in fifteen minutes anyway, and it looks like we're stopping at the apothecary shop before we go, so scoot."

One of Chaos's eyes popped open again. She lifted her cheek and her mouth twisted disapprovingly, but Carissa folded the 'kerchief and placed it on the dresser. If she wanted her blanket back, she'd have to get up now.

Chaos sat up and thrust her hands in the air for a stretch. She yawned and covered her face with her hands. Clutching the chocolate cosmos for support, she stood.

Carissa let her play out the dramatics while she grabbed the bags. A small, pink, makeup bag sat on top, a mauve one for books and other items her parents had loaned her from her grandfather's study rested in the middle, and at the base of the other two sat a large, red rolling suitcase for clothes. Carissa should have checked that they were stable before snatching the handle of the rolling luggage because the pink bag quivered and fell to the floor.

Carissa groaned, hoping none of the powders or foundation had spilled inside. She had no time to check. Instead, Carissa repositioned the luggage. Then, using her elf-light to ease the weight, she rolled the bags downstairs behind her. Chaos followed as Carissa knew she would.

"That's something, indeed." Nan's voice traveled from the kitchen.

Carissa turned the corner at the bottom of the stairway to see Nan and Sal seated, each with teacups steaming on saucers in front of them.

Sal fiddled with the cup handle. "I wouldn't ask it—I know how important this mission is, but—" Sal stopped, looking in Carissa's direction.

Elves were supposed to be light on their feet, but that darn pink bag kept slipping. It fell to the floor the same moment Sal's slender elfkin ears heard it lose the battle with gravity.

Carissa picked it up.

"Sorry," she said. "What have I interrupted?"

Sal stood. "Well, I...um..." Sal glanced over at the table and grabbed a paper bag that was rolled up with a rubber band in the center. "Got the herbs. Your nan said you had some in the garden and she was nice enough to let me take a fair amount."

Carissa couldn't help but smile whenever Sal did. A grin on his joyful face was infectious. But she did keep a skeptical eye out this time. "Oh? Which ones did you need?"

Sal's voice squeaked as if straining against the nonchalant tone he was taking, "Just some ginger root, peppermint, a little chamomile tea."

"And some licorice root," Nan added as she lifted her cup to curled lips.

Carissa suspected Nan knew something that Sal was afraid of telling her. Even Chaos caught on to it. The nature fae crossed her arms as Carissa's eyebrow raised. The licorice root was one of Hela's favorite, especially since her pregnancy, but it was readily available in Vale—as were the other herbs.

Carissa played along. "Is Hela having morning sickness?"

"No, uh..." Sal scratched his head like he was unsure what to say next.

"He wants to go with you," Nan intervened.

Carissa squinted as if trying to literally see his point. "To the marina?"

"On your trip," Sal said.

"Sal, why don't you help Cari with her bags? You two have your elf-light, and now that she's up early, you have time to spare. It's a nice morning, too. Walk with her and explain on the way."

Carissa wanted to argue that the marina was on the other side of the island and that even Cari never traveled that far on foot. Part of Carissa believed Nan was purposely choosing to get out of her promise to drive her, but an even more conscious part of her knew that there was something more to Nan's request. Sal needed her help.

He had already brushed past her and was maneuvering the luggage outside the door before she could protest. Chaos shrugged before taking her usual seat on Carissa's shoulder. She had no reason to complain. She didn't have to walk.

Not that it was hard for Carissa. With her elf-light, she not only caught up with Sal in a second, but their steps synced into a magically quick-footed rhythm. Sal began speaking and stopped to set the troublesome pink bag steady again.

"I know what you're thinking, Cari. I mean, I think I do, but Hela really did send me to fetch those herbs from you—yesterday, actually."

Carissa nodded. "We closed the shop a little early. I understand."

"No, that's not it. I couldn't work up the nerve to see you."

Carissa's ears twitched, and she looked at Sal, whose eyes were concentrated on the ground. "Why?"

"'Cause I know this trip is important to you, and I know you don't want an elfkin in the way, but I have to ask you anyway if I can come along."

Carissa did not want to repeat the same question, but she again wondered why Sal would even want to make a dangerous, long voyage to a land of powerful fae who were also sometimes known for being temperamental. It wasn't like Sal to want to leave his employ to face danger, especially when his service was needed given Hela's pregnancy. It was dangerous enough running all over Moss Hill and Vale finding foods to match Hela's cravings. It was even less like Sal to be so nervous about asking Carissa about anything.

"Sal, it's dangerous."

"I know," he said quickly, "but I have to go. I owe it to my parents."

"Your parents?"

Sal lifted the pink bag and strapped it onto his shoulder. The sight of it did not match the seriousness of his look.

"Fudge told me that my parents died on the shores of Rhys Dwfen."

"Rhys Dwfen…I remember reading about that in my grandfather's books. It's an island of elfkin, isn't it? Is that where you and Fudge are from?"

"It is. Though I was a baby when I left, so I can't say I remember it at all."

"Your parents died when you were a baby? How did they…" Carissa stopped herself. Sal's pained eyes told her she was only hurting him more with each word.

Still, he explained, "A ship crashed on the shore when we were picnicking. I was just a wee one but walking, wandering off catching butterflies or some such thing. Somehow, I escaped, but my parents were in the path of the vessel…."

"Oh, Sal, I'm so sorry." Carissa put a hand on his arm.

He straightened and wiped away a tear. "Fudge, he's my uncle, you see. He brought me to Moss Hill, where Master Rolin took me in."

Fudge? Sal's uncle? That explained their similarity in appearance, but none of the vast differences in their personalities. It also didn't explain why Fudge had left Sal in Vale instead of raising his nephew himself. Sal was probably better off for it.

"I want to see it—Rhys Dwfen. Pay my respects at my parents' graves."

"I understand, Sal, but I don't think we're stopping there."

"It's on the way. I asked Rolin."

"And he told you?"

Sal reddened, lowering his voice. "I may have seen a map in his study. I wasn't trying to look. I know the location of Hy Brasil is a secret. I wouldn't tell no one, I swear. But I can't help what I saw. And Rhys Dwfen is definitely on the way."

"Doesn't mean that we'll stop. I'm sorry, Sal, but I don't control the *Scuabtuinne's* route."

"You'll need supplies, won't you? Have you heard about the island before, Cari? Friendliest port in the world is the home of the Children of the Deep Rhys. They have travelers go to every island in the world to barter, and they trade all those goods with visitors. They've got booths set up for miles on weekends—biggest seaside marketplace you've ever seen."

The wind picked up, sending a lock of Carissa's red hair onto her teeth as she smiled. She pushed the strands away. "I'm sure they are. I've no doubt in elfkin hospitality."

She couldn't stop using Hela's nickname for the Rhys Dwfen faeries: elfkin. Sal and Fudge were the only such fae on the island, and they didn't seem to mind the name an elf-woman has so lovingly given them as a child. But the effect was that Carissa knew very little about their true heritage or their people. She wished she could promise Sal they'd take him, especially when he made his final plea.

"They're my people and I don't even know them, Cari. Even if we just pass by the island.... I have to see it. And the fact is, I already sent a letter to my cousins. It should arrive by the time we get there."

Carissa shook her head. Sal's passion was moving, even if he'd acted rashly. Besides, the way he described it, she was tempted to see the island herself.

"I can ask Logan, but that's all I can do. I can't promise you."

Sal beamed. Despite the way the pink bag jostled, he shook her hand with vigor. "Thank you! You won't regret having me aboard. I'll earn my ticket. Help out, cook, scrub, or whatever you need me to do."

"Or take a vacation, Sal. Goodness knows you deserve one." Carissa blurted it without thinking, but it was a good idea.

Sal wasn't the one who had to draft a speech that would move the Tuatha de Danann to keep the realms open, help them create more Moss Hills all over the world, and eventually reveal the fae presence to all of mankind. There was no reason he couldn't have a relaxing trip. There was no reason everyone else couldn't relax while Carissa carried the weight of Moss Hill's future on her shoulders.

"I'm not sure I can take a vacation just now," Sal said.

Their elf-light speed had brought them across the island within a half hour. They rounded the corner of the last street up to the beach and began their descent to the shore. Sal fumbled with the bags as the terrain became more rugged.

Taking the pink bag off Sal's shoulders and lifting the handheld mauve one off the rolling cart, Carissa attempted to raise all the luggage herself. Sal held a hand up on the last one, insisting, as a gentleman, to help with the heftiest suitcase.

He added, "That's not what I mean, Cari, I'm happy to help."

But the gesture did more than make Carissa appreciative of his kindness. It reminded her that Sal hadn't come prepared for a trip. As they walked down to the port, Carissa could see the crewmen hoisting luggage onto the ship.

"Sal, did you bring any bags? We're leaving in less than an hour. You'd better hurry and pack if you want to join us."

Sal's hand wavered as he scratched an ear. "Well, actually, I should mention…" Sal's sentence left off as they came within feet of the pier.

"Cari!" a feminine voice squealed. Hela, in a flowing, blue dress—with a baby bump showing—dodged crewmen down the wood walkway with an awkwardness and agility only an elf mother-to-be could manage. All her shining white teeth showed as she embraced Carissa into a hug. She pulled away, beaming.

"Isn't this exciting? Hy Brasil, did you ever think we'd get to see it?"

Carissa shook her head. "Um, no, I...I'm sorry, what are you doing here?"

"This is where we're boarding, isn't it?" As Hela turned to face the ramp, Carissa glanced questioningly at Sal.

Sal cleared his throat. "Erm, I should've mentioned: Miss Hela and Master Fen are requesting to come along, too."

"Not requesting." Fen appeared behind his wife. His tone was gentle, explaining, "My father-in-law has issued a command that I go."

"Rolin wants you to go to Hy Brasil?"

"As the official bard of Vale, I'm qualified to recite an oral history of our people."

Bard of Vale, so that was Fen's position. Carissa had always known him to be a uniquely talented poet, artist, sculptor, and singer, but she'd never known exactly what he did for a living, except that he was the son-in-law of the head of the Elf Council. Carissa could see why Rolin might want to send an elf to Hy Brasil, but she would have thought it better to include her own father, who was the official historian. As to why Rolin thought it wise to send Hela, that was beyond all reasoning.

Carissa could not let it go unchallenged. "The trip could be dangerous. Hela, in your condition—"

"It's perfect! My baby will be infused with magic in Hy Brasil. Even the herbs in the land of the Tuatha de Danann are said to have magic-enhancing properties. My child might become the most magical elf of our time."

"Hela," Carissa didn't mean to shout, but it took that much to make Hela snap out of it, "that won't matter if you have any complications on the way. Surely your father wouldn't just let you go."

Hela barely batted an eye. "I'm a grown woman, Cari. It's my decision. And I'm not without my own skill in magic, though I might not use it often."

Case in point, Hela used her elf-light to levitate the last of her bags onto the ship. She must have brought at least thirteen of them, which was impressive. Though the excessive amount of luggage was outdone by the magic Hela used to lift them. Carissa felt the weight of her own pink bag shifting. *Was the bag defective?*

She looked at Fen for help persuading his wife. His defeated headshake told her this was a losing battle. Carissa tried anyway, for the baby's sake.

"Hela, what about morning sickness? It'll be far worse out at sea."

"Sal brought the herbs, didn't he?" Hela looked to Sal, who nodded. Self-pleased, Hela used her elf-light to take not only Sal's load, including Carissa's rolling cart, but also the bags in Carissa's arms. They floated up the portside as Hela said, "There, see? You're an apothecary, you can certainly help with any sickness I feel on the trip."

"And if we get attacked?" Carissa asked.

"You sound like Fen. I was at the last Elf Council meeting, and I can tell you no one knows the real purpose of this trip except for us. Everyone thinks this is just a vacation. What better way to keep up the charade than having me along?"

No one knew there was a secret purpose to their journey *until* Hela squealed that fact here in the marina, but it wasn't fair to be angry with her for that since it was early in the morning and there was no one around but the travelers.

Yet, secrets weren't always well-kept, especially in Moss Hill.

Hela's twisted logic was beyond arguing. As much as Carissa wanted to convince her to stay, she knew from experience that once Hela got an idea into her mind, there was no way to take it out. The only person who could force her to stay was the captain, and by order of Raven Corvus, he had to let anyone on whom Carissa said was okay. Still, she tried to make the argument.

Hela was deaf to it. "If he let those three nature faeries come, I can't see why he wouldn't let me aboard."

"Chaos is different," Carissa began, stopping a second later to realize what Hela had said. "Three fae?"

She looked up, sure enough, two little pairs of eyes peeked over the pink makeup bag, disappearing over the ship's side. Carissa looked to Chaos, still asleep on her shoulder. She wanted to jostle her awake, but a hand tapped Carissa's other shoulder.

Cameron appeared behind her, eyebrows furrowed. He watched Hela and Fen board the ship, then he looked back toward the beach.

"You haven't seen Reg, have you?" he asked.

"No, why, did he say he was coming this morning?"

To see them off is what she meant, though at this point she wouldn't be surprised if he was coming on the journey, too. Cam shook his head. His eyes settled on hers.

"He never showed last night."

"Maren said he was busy at the office."

"Yeah, but not saying goodbye at all? I don't know. That doesn't seem like him."

"Did you try calling him?"

"Way too early." Cam tried for a smile, "I'm sure he's fine. Are you ready to go?"

Before Carissa could answer, a voice called out, "Wait! Wait for me!"

Tabitha half ran half flew across the beach and to the pier. Her boyfriend, Mr. Otto Crimbal, followed behind, holding the bags. The changeling man and woman thrust their belongings into the arms of the last crewman standing on the dock.

"Don't forget *us*, you mean," he said in his usual surly tone.

Cam leaned in and whispered, "Are they both going with us?"

Carissa gave up by now. "Sure, why not?"

After all, what was a secret mission without roughly half a dozen of Carissa's closest friends?

Chapter 3

One-Upmanship

To be on the other end of Chaos's wagging finger was not, as Carissa imagined, a pleasant situation in which to find oneself. Hiya and Cynth dodged sparks of faerie dust shooting from the nature faerie's fingertips, but they would not budge from the porthole window. The window was a beautiful round circle of polished wood and silver, as exquisite as the rest of the room.

It was larger than Carissa had thought it would be, two executive suites—Carissa's and Cameron's—connected with a door. Carissa couldn't help but explore both. Cameron was not in his room at the moment, but his suitcase lay on his bed. His room mirrored hers, with a sofa and a table secured to the floor, and two chairs of sturdy, polished wood. In her own room, Carissa studied the intricate carvings of crashing waves that ran down the legs of each piece of furniture.

When Chaos had exhausted herself with the hand-waving gestures—her equivalent of shouting—Cynth crossed her arms. Hiya plugged his ears, and the whole competition in stubbornness threatened to repeat itself.

"All right, all of you just stop." Carissa closed her eyes, pinched the bridge of her nose, and said, "Hiya, Cynth, this trip could be dangerous. Go home, or I swear I will use my Tuatha de Danann magic to send you back myself."

She hoped they couldn't see through her bluff. Less than practiced in such magic, Carissa had no way of knowing whether she could pull off a spell over long distances. Apparently, the nature faeries didn't care. Hiya thrust an index finger at Chaos, his eyes pleading with Carissa. Chaos crossed her arms and looked at Carissa as if demanding the correct response.

Chaos scooted to the portal window and placed both palms on the glass. Either the water had caught her attention, or she was tired of giving this conversation any more notice.

Hiya continued his teary-eyed accusation against a no-longer-interested Chaos. Cynth had taken to merely standing with crossed arms and an even more cross expression. Though the watery eyes were there, too. The message was clear: they were angry she had wanted Chaos along, but not them.

Carissa felt her resolve breaking, but she tried to stand firm. "That's different, Chaos has some of Raven's magic, she's—"

Cynth flew in her face. The sprite gestured between Carissa and herself to signal their bond. Then, down went her hand, palm toward the floor as if measuring Carissa as she was when she was young.

"Yes, I know. And I appreciate that you've always been there for me since I was a little girl."

Now Cynth joined Hiya in pointing angrily at Chaos. Carissa got the message. Hiya and Cynth had been there through thick and thin, even when the other sprites in her garden had not, or when Carissa's parents had not. They'd journeyed with her when she went to college.

Chaos had only met Carissa a year or so ago. It was not the same lifelong bond Hiya and Cynth shared with Carissa. But that was precisely why she wanted her two faerie friends safe.

"Listen, it's not that I don't want you with me," Carissa began.

That was all Hiya and Cynth needed to hear. Cynth hovered above Carissa, giving her a pat on the head as if forgiving her for her foolishness. She and Hiya flew back to the makeup bag, taking out the berries and herbs they'd snuck on board as their "luggage." Chaos threw up her hands as she made her way to Carissa's shoulder.

That was that.

Two spirited sprites, one pregnant elf and her doting husband, a helpful elfkin, and two changelings who were strange even by Mossie standards had somehow stowed away on this trip, and there was only one way to stop them.

With Chaos taking a seat on her shoulder, Carissa walked out of the cabin, wrestling her conscience all the way to the deck. If she told Logan to kick them all off the ship, then by captain's orders they would have to leave. They would be angry with her, of course. But it would be for their own good, wouldn't it?

She reached the railing and looked over Moss Hill's marina while her thoughts drifted. This was the last time she would see Moss Hill—at least for a while. It was beautiful with the sunlight dancing in waves along its shores. The scene jumped, or rather, the ship jolted forward, causing Carissa to grab the rail. Chaos fled to the air.

"Well, I guess it's too late." Carissa looked at Chaos. "Anyone on board is going all the way to Hy Brasil."

Part of her was glad.

***

THE *SCUABTUINNE* SLICED through the water as if it were a wave itself. Outside on the deck, Carissa could see no cause of the water that had splashed on her window earlier, unless a crewman had taken the fact that everyone was unpacking in their cabins as an opportunity to clean the ship. The vessel was spotless the moment they'd arrived, so that didn't seem likely.

Chaos flew up to the porthole window only to fly down, shaking her head. The eye-rolling told Carissa that inside Hiya and Cynth were still causing a ruckus with their unpacking. They'd have to come out soon for breakfast, but for the time being, they were safe in the cabin.

It was a good thing since the foggy morning was turning to a stormy day. Carissa had to stop to admire the sight from the starboard side, then she walked to the stern, looking for Cameron.

Instead of her boyfriend, she found the crewmen. They barely noticed her except for the occasional head bow in recognition of her presence. Though they were all druids, these men wore no signs of magic or otherworldly charms. Instead, they donned blue pants and white, hooded, button-down shirts, which could pass in any port for expected human attire. Alone, none would stand out in a crowd, but together, they were easily identified as part of a uniform crew.

Logan wore a blue-gray shirt and matching pants that reminded Carissa of the tunic of the Prince of Sidhe and Elves and Cameron's slickest business suit combined. If there was a symbol marking him as captain, Carissa had yet to recognize it. But the three-quarter sleeve with silver drawstrings at the collar, designed to show off his brawny chest, made him stand out from the others. Today he wore a navy jacket atop his usual ensemble. The reflective waves across the top might be his captain's stripes.

It was also how Carissa spotted him as she walked past the stern and back to the main deck along the portside. The sun glinted off the captain's jacket with as much glare as it did on the silver dress of the woman speaking with the captain. Carissa stepped behind the mast on instinct. She didn't mean to hide, but eavesdropping was involuntary for her—both as an elf and as a Mossie.

The woman, a tall, blue-eyed, reddish-blonde with flawless, pearl-white skin spoke in a melodic accent Carissa did not recognize. "You must keep it secret. If they knew they might turn on you."

"But the flame might not be enough," Logan responded.

"Water is stronger than fire," the woman said, "and there are as many of us as the ocean is wide."

"I would not ask the water fae for favors. And they would not grant me any if I asked," Logan's voice shook with no small amount of bitterness.

"Do you need something?"

A male voice too close to Carissa's ear made her jump. The movement stopped the captain's conversation and shifted both sets of eyes onto her. Chaos returned to Carissa's shoulder in support—or perhaps to hide her embarrassment. Carissa straightened and tried to appear nonchalant.

"I was just looking for my boyfriend, Cameron Larke."

The red-headed druid crewman nodded. "He is at the bow, Miss Shae, speaking with the dreg."

Carissa's eyes flared. Since the man turned, he missed it. She followed him, growing angrier with each step. Dreg? As in the dregs of society? Who did he mean? Surely it wasn't Sal, who may have been a servant in an elf's home but was more gentleman than most.

"You are wrong about him," Carissa called out as they rounded the corner.

Past the helm, Cameron conversed with a burly man Carissa recognized as Gerard Buxley—the kelpie who had taken a human identity out of hope for a human love with a woman who did not even know she loved him. But in his desperation to be human, this water horse faerie had also aided and abetted a druid criminal.

"I hope I'm wrong," the druid whispered as he walked away, adding as his shoulder brushed hers, "but I fear I'm not."

Carissa turned her attention to Cameron, who had taken an all-too-relaxed stance against the railing considering how menacingly straight and tall the kelpie stood inches from him.

Whatever they'd been talking about before, they were quiet now, staring an extra second longer at each other before turning their attention toward her.

"What are you doing here?" Carissa asked.

Gerard did not shrink from her gaze. "Part of my sentence."

Cameron came away from the railing. "It's all right, Cari. Mr. Buxley, uh, Gerard, came with Fen. Apparently, the Elf Council thought he deserved a second chance."

"You knew about this?" Carissa asked.

"N—"

"No," Gerard interrupted Cameron. "He met me here on the promenade and has been kind enough to believe me. As he should." Gerard stepped forward.

Involuntarily, Carissa flinched. Kelpies were as massive in human form as they were in fae form, but Gerard did not show any violence toward her. Instead, he held his palms up to calm her.

Cameron did the same, only he gently touched Carissa's shoulder. "He was warning me about the water fae. He says that many of them are loyal to the Ocean Reaper and in turn to Niall Shae."

Niall Shae. The name had been on her mind since she'd discovered she had a cousin, however distant, who was part Tuatha de Danann like herself. Unlike her, he had visions of a world in which humans were controlled by the fae—or removed altogether. He had no human side but had taken a human surname, her family's name, though no one knew why. Maybe it had been for the same reason Gerard had chosen a last name: camouflage.

Gerard, whose size and stature made it hard to blend in, had enough fondness for humans to sneer at the mention of Niall Shae.

"The unseelie may not all agree with Maeb's heir, but many do whatever they see is in their best interest," Gerard said.

Carissa leaned into Cameron. "The Ocean Reaper is in custody in Moss Hill. MacLir will banish him to the world beyond the first chance he gets. I don't see how it's in any water fae's best interest to serve him anymore." Even as she said it, the cold rushing through her told her otherwise.

Gerard confirmed her fear. "Warren Druvall is not in Moss Hill. He is on the sea."

"What?"

"He left on the king's ship this morning with Raven. Reg oversaw it personally on order of MacLir," Cameron explained.

Carissa frowned. That explained why Reg wasn't around recently. But why would MacLir want Warren on the ocean? As the Tuatha de Danann in charge of the world beyond, MacLir was needed to banish a reaper, but why wouldn't he just come to Moss Hill himself to do the task there? Why risk putting the Ocean Reaper back on the water?

Cameron answered as if reading her mind. "Warren was under employment with the King of Sidhe and Elves. They're taking him back to Tir-Na-Nog to face sentencing by the king."

Carissa put it together. "It would be a breach in propriety for the Sidhe Council to charge him instead of the king himself. But on the seas, the water fae working for Niall might try to free Warren."

Cameron squeezed her shoulder reassuringly. "With Raven on board, I doubt anyone would try to attack."

Carissa thought back to the woman she'd seen just moments ago. The sheen on her dress hinted that she was a water fae, and she had a confidence that bordered on arrogance. "Those loyal to him might still try."

Gerard grunted. "Few water fae are loyal to anyone. Their nature is as changeable as the sea."

"Is yours?" Carissa asked so bluntly Cameron pulled at his collar to show his agitation.

"If it weren't, I would not be helping you."

As the winds picked up, Carissa, Cameron, and Gerard all turned away from the railing. A figure approached, calling Carissa's name. Captain Logan waved for them to take shelter inside.

As they left, Gerard muttered loud enough for only her elfish ears to hear him, "But the winds are blowing in your favor, Mossie, and I've my own reasons to want your side to win."

Chapter 4

Muddy Waters

"You'll catch your death in this dreich weather. Best stay indoors till it blows over," Logan suggested.

In the captain's quarters, Carissa and Cameron warmed themselves by a green, faerie fire. Carissa did not know much about sailing, but she was sure a fire on a ship was not a typical sight. Chaos took herself to the brink of the light. Carissa called her back, worried she might burn herself, but the nature faerie stopped just short of the flame. Her little fingers pressed against an invisible shielding. Glass. The fae fire swirled so as not to touch anything, including the fae-formed glass encasing it. Logan caught her and Chaos admiring it.

"That's the heart of the ship—the reason the *Scuabtuinne* is the fastest ship on the sea."

Cameron raised his eyebrows. "Faerie fire? Don't any of the other fae ships use it?"

"Not *'faerie fire'*," Logan mocked. "An Immortal Flame."

"A Tuatha de Danann's fire," Carissa clarified.

"Your own?" Cam asked.

Handing a mug of some brownish liquid to Cameron and Carissa, Logan answered, "Though this boat was originally Manann MacLir's, today there's not a part of this ship that is not the handiwork of Lugh."

He patted the ship like a child. It was his child, Carissa supposed, since Logan seemed to enjoy a bachelor's life and had no family other than his crew. Ignoring the third-person reference to himself that Lugh had made, Carissa pondered instead whether this was the flame he'd spoken about with that mysterious woman.

The hairs on Carissa's neck stood, likely because of the strength of whatever was in her cup. After one sip, she coughed so hard Logan had to take the drink from her. Cameron patted her back, but she could tell he was struggling with his own breath. Logan laughed.

"That's real faerie fire. At least, that's what we call it on this ship. Fae Fire Ale is a mix of ingredients we've found from our voyages. You have to develop a taste for it."

"Or a tolerance," Cam whispered while tilting the glass to examine the contents.

Carissa chuckled now that she could breathe. Part of her worried, though. It was too early in the day for drinking, much less for a captain to be doing so. It seemed to catch Chaos's attention, too.

The sprite followed Logan as he set the mugs back on the bar. He took one for himself before he rejoined Carissa and Cameron. In his chair by the hearth, his gigantic stature competed with the fire for which was the more intimidating sight. Would all the Tuatha de Danann look so fierce? Or would they be more like Manann or Macara, who had chosen to blend in with human society?

"You know, my love of the sea started at a very young age, even before I met MacLir."

"You aren't his son?" Carissa asked.

"Adopted," Cam leaned toward her and whispered.

Since when did he know so much about Logan's history? Carissa wondered how long he'd stayed last night listening to Logan's stories.

"I may have been five or six when a hurricane swallowed up my whole town. Of course, everyone was runnin' about all affright, but I was brave in the face of such terrible danger. MacLir thought so, too, and so he took me in."

Carissa felt a mix of compassion for Logan's loss and disdain for the bravado with which he told his story. She gave a half-hearted smile, noting how Cameron's eyes were glued to Logan with sympathy. He might have been absorbed in the self-aggrandizing story, but Carissa had no interest in feeding Logan's ego. Besides, the story left her with questions.

"Couldn't the Tuatha de Danann in your town do anything to stop the hurricane?" She recalled how Raven seemed to create a storm of her own when she'd arrived in Moss Hill.

Logan's eyes flicked down. His lips opened and sealed again. The lines around his eyes deepened, and Carissa surmised that something about her question had upset him.

Cameron sat forward.

"Logan, Lugh in the myths, he didn't live with his parents. And his father was Fomorian, so even if he'd lived with them…"

"A Fomorian?" That's right. Carissa reminded herself that Logan had said this back in Moss Hill. But except for his reference in the pub, Carissa could not find the word in her memory. She said, "I know you mentioned them before, but, who were the Fomorians?"

Cameron answered, "We read about them, remember? They were almost as powerful as the Tuatha de Danann but more aggressive. They fought so much, they were driven out of Ireland and even then, they continued with the infighting. Legend says there aren't any left on earth anymore, except possibly deep in the oceans." Cameron glanced at Logan as if he just realized he'd said too much. "I'm sorry. That must be painful to hear."

Logan waved it off, literally. He took a drink from the Fire Ale. Carissa looked at Logan with newfound sympathy. Somehow, she felt apologizing for the question would only make him feel worse. So, she let the silence linger.

It wasn't long before Logan regained his smile, asking Cameron, "So, you've read the stories of Lugh?"

Carissa's eyebrow rose again. She wanted to like him, but was he really referring to himself in the third person? Was anyone that ego-centric?

"Yes, shortly after you came. You're incredibly impressive in them." The awe returned to Cameron's eyes.

"The tales are unbelievable, aren't they? Yet, they're all true. Have you read the one where—"

Carissa rolled her eyes, not even wanting to hear the rest. But as she looked away, she spotted Chaos at Logan's private bar, bending over the side of one of the mugs to sneak a sip. Carissa used her elf-light to send a little electric magic through the air to zap the nature faerie in the bum. It went unnoticed by Cameron, who was so enthralled with Logan's story.

Chaos jumped back and rubbed her bottom. Carissa subtly shook her head no, for goodness knows what would have happened to the sprite if she'd drunk the ale. Chaos scowled at the reprimand. Then she smiled sneakily and held two hands up toward the mug. Carissa's eyes widened. Chaos's faerie dust floated the cup toward Logan.

"No," Carissa mouthed.

But Chaos would not listen. The cup began to tilt over Logan's head. Nudging Cameron, Carissa lifted her chin in the direction of the looming disaster.

His eyes ballooned, and, in one swift motion, he rose to fetch the mug before Chaos spilled the Fae Fire all over the captain's face. Logan, who hadn't noticed a thing before Cameron's strange lunge forward, stopped speaking and blinked.

Carissa caught his attention by standing. "We ought to get back to our cabin."

Logan squinted before glancing at Cameron. He'd made it back to the bar. For good measure, Cameron took a swig of the liquid. He coughed.

"That's just so good," he struggled to say. Chaos shook in his closed fist as his body racked with several deeper coughs.

She zapped him once, but Cameron only switched her from one hand to another.

Logan's mouth widened to show all his teeth. "You must join me after my watch tonight and we'll drink while I share more of my many adventures."

"Yes," Cam's voice cracked, "I'll be there, but we need to finish unpacking, so…"

"Certainly. Best go before the rain catches you." Logan nodded to the window.

Soft droplets fell against the glass and traveled down in streaks. The drizzle had already started, but if they hurried, they might make it back before the rain. Cameron held a surly sprite in his hands as Carissa opened the door.

"What were you thinking?" Carissa scolded as they left.

Unappreciative of the hand Cameron cupped overhead to shield her from the raindrops, Chaos crossed her arms and turned her head away from them. She stayed like that until they reached the cabin. Then Cameron let go of her, and she flew to the porthole window to sulk.

Hiya and Cynth, who'd opened every bit of luggage, popped out from underneath Carissa's clothing to see what was the matter. Cameron shrugged off his wet jacket and set it on the bed. Carissa shook her head and put it on the hook by the door.

"I don't think Chaos meant any real harm. Logan is nice enough. Even if she spilled it, he'd probably just laugh it off. Don't be angry with her."

"I'm just as angry with you," Carissa said.

"Me? Why?" Cameron's eyebrows reached a new height as his mouth dropped.

"You didn't have to agree to sit up all night drinking with Logan."

"We won't be all night, and, wait, what is she saying?" He pointed at Chaos, who was signing like mad in the window.

Carissa didn't have the patience to interpret every word. "Something about 'Logan is not a hero,' he's pretending or something. Chaos, just stop. As annoying as he is, you know that's not true."

"Annoying? What happened? Chaos loved him yesterday," Cameron said, to which Chaos stuck out her tongue.

Carissa sighed. She turned back to Cameron, intent on not letting him change the subject.

"That's not the point. I don't want you drinking on the deck of a ship in the middle of the night out in the ocean. There are water fae everywhere, and you're only..." Her fingertips covered her mouth unconsciously.

"Only human?" Cameron finished her thought with the quietest tone she'd ever heard him use.

She closed her eyes. She hadn't meant to be hurtful. She only wanted to protect him. She was scared enough traveling so far from home without risking Cameron, too. This trip was making it difficult to keep her loved ones out of danger.

"Cam, I—"

He pulled his jacket off the rack and slid it on, saying, "I'm part water fae, too, you know. It may be far into my past from some distant relative, but it is there. I'm trying to find myself on this journey, Cari. I thought of all people, you would understand."

Having hurt him far more than she thought possible, Carissa watched him leave with just as much regret. Between the rain, the angry nature faerie, and the offended boyfriend, this trip was starting off about as well as a life raft with a hole in the middle. She had a sinking feeling it was only going to get worse.

***

AFTER TWO HOURS of unpacking, which should have been a fifteen-minute job, Carissa hoped the knock rousing her from her thoughts was Cameron returning. Instead, she opened the door to greet Hela. The radiant mother-to-be wore a sunny expression that brightened the gray drizzle outside.

Twirling her umbrella, Hela said, "Brunch has been on for an hour, and we didn't see you. Aren't you coming?"

Brunch. Carissa just then realized the twisting pain in her stomach was more than just nerves. That explained why Cameron hadn't already returned. She'd likely find him in the dining hall. *Had he really been so upset with her that he would attend the brunch by himself?* She wanted to frown, but since there was no reason to upset Hela with her personal problems, Carissa nodded and smiled.

"Yes, I was just about to make my way there," she fibbed.

"Perfect." Hela linked her arm with Carissa and pulled her out the door before she could react.

Never ones to miss a meal, the sprites rushed past the doorframe just before the door snapped closed. They settled onto the lacy bundles of Hela's ruffled, pink frock. This was a fancier dress than she'd worn in the morning. Knowing Hela, she'd make at least three outfit changes a day, saving the most extravagant pieces for the dinners.

The brunch was a much more informal affair than Hela's dress made it out to be, but a more lavish one than Carissa had expected. The dishes were an international mix of fae delicacies, ones that Carissa only knew because of her parents. Their ambassadorial travels meant that they'd brought home Scandinavian cloudberry ambrosia, English huallepen sausages, Spanish barnacle tree eggs, and much more. Each entrée was nested in its own magically re-filling cornucopias. Carissa was grateful to see tropical juices and water instead of Faerie Fire for drinks.

She was even happier to see Cameron at the end of the buffet chatting with Fen. Hela walked straight to her husband, forcing Carissa to follow. It dawned on Carissa that this may have been Hela's intention all along. Though she acted oblivious, Hela had always been aware of others' romantic relationships.

Once at the buffet, Hela pulled Fen away on the excuse that they should keep Sal company. Carissa watched them leave, noting that Sal, for once, was seated and enjoying a meal instead of serving anyone. Hiya, Cynth, and Chaos were doing the same. Carissa wasn't sure when they'd left Hela to skim the buffet table, but they were hopping up and down the length of it, from one dish to another, using mint leaves as plates.

Carissa grinned, keeping a hopeful smile as she turned back to Cameron. To her relief, he didn't look angry. Instead, he reached a hand out to her.

"I'm sorry," he said.

"*I'm* sorry." Carissa squeezed his fingers. "I should've realized this trip was about more to you than just our mission in Hy Brasil."

"And I know you're worried about keeping everyone safe, but this isn't all on your shoulders." He let a laugh escape. "We might all be here for our own reasons, but for all of us, the most important of those reasons is to help you."

He left Carissa to gather her food while he took a seat at the table next to Fen. Sal stood out of courtesy and Cam had to remind him he was not there to serve. He reddened as he lowered himself back into his chair.

Carissa bit her lip gently. She'd almost forgotten about Sal. Cameron was right that they were all there for different reasons. She'd allowed her mission to occupy so much of her thoughts that she almost forgot about Sal's request.

Before heading to the buffet, she found Logan at the portside door. There was that woman with him again, though they were walking away from each other. Whatever she said seemed to upset Logan. Carissa could see the scowl spreading over his face. She hurried to make it to them before they parted. Just a step outside the door, she caught them both.

"Captain," Carissa said.

Logan and the mysterious woman faced her. The ever-amiable captain persona returned to his face. He gestured from Carissa to the woman.

"Cari, I'd like you to meet Beathan, the head of my ocean guard."

The woman dipped her head low in recognition of the introduction.

Carissa bowed awkwardly in return. "Ocean guard?"

"The water fae who see you safely through the ocean," Beathan answered.

Captain Logan cleared his throat. "They take shifts protecting the water below. Though the *Scuabtuinne* can hold its own in battle, it is always good to have friends around us."

"What type of water fae are you?" Carissa knew it was blunt. She didn't mean to offend Beathan, but there was something about this woman she found strange. The way Beathan shifted at the question only made her seem more suspicious.

"One with a great deal of responsibility," Logan answered for her with no further explanation.

Beathan bowed, saying, "I'll take my leave."

"It was nice to meet you," Carissa said, but Beathan was already walking away.

The water fae walked straight to the railing. Then she dived over. Carissa's mouth opened, stopping just short of yelling, *"Look out!"* as the water splashed all the way up to the deck windows. But the fall was intentional. Carissa couldn't see the whole transformation but saw that the woman's legs turned a silvery color that blended with her dress as she jumped. Her water fae nature must have made leaping into the ocean a natural action.

"Did you have a question for me?"

The captain brought Carissa's attention back. She blinked, stumbling a bit before finding the right words.

"I, um, yes, I was wondering if we could make a stop at the Island of Rhys Dwfen."

"The Deep Rhys? I had no plans to go there, why?"

"It's personal…a friend, well, it's very important to my friend Sal, who joined us this morning."

"Oh, yes, we have a few islanders aboard, don't we? You know our mission is sensitive, Cari."

"I know, but it means everything to Sal. It's where his parents died."

Logan laid a hand on her shoulder. "Say no more. I will talk to my chief druid and to Beathan. I can't promise you anything, but if we need to stop for supplies, perhaps we can make it to Rhys Dwfen for a day or so."

"Thank you, Captain." Carissa stepped back indoors while Captain Logan walked toward the bow of the ship.

Inside, she took her plate and filled it, though not as overflowing as Chaos, Hiya, and Cynth had made their plates. She and the faeries headed for the table to sit beside Sal. He leaned forward, and Carissa held a hand out to stop him. If she didn't insist he stay seated, Carissa knew that Sal would push her chair in for her, ask her what drink she'd like, and wait on her hand and foot. He sat as Cameron pushed her chair in. Sal turned the same shade of elderberry juice in Carissa's cup.

"Relax. It's your vacation, remember?" Carissa laughed.

Sal chuckled, too. "And what a vacation it's been. Everything here is so wonderful!" He stretched his arms out as if encompassing the whole room.

It had rained most of the morning, which she'd almost interpreted as an inauspicious start to their voyage. But now, with Sal beaming, Hela laughing, Chaos, Hiya, and Cynth swiping berries from everyone's plates, and Cameron reaching for her hand, Carissa could allow herself to believe that all would be smooth sailing from here on out. It was going to be a successful journey, even if the weather was taking a turn for the worse.

Chapter 5

Crime of the Century

The table reserved for Tabitha and Otto sat empty during the brunch. At first, Carissa assumed that they had simply eaten and left. But Hela said she had not seen Tabitha at all since they'd first boarded. Her story of what had happened at that time seemed even stranger.

"She said to that water fae woman something like, 'It's just a room change, and no one is even using this one.' Then Otto said something like he knows who she really is and that the room change is the least of her worries. The woman was so angry." Hela shuddered. "She called them both 'insane' and, well, you know Tabitha…"

Carissa knew both Tabitha and Hela enough to take Hela's words with a grain of salt. The elf-woman was not very fond of the changeling. When they'd first met, Tabitha had been suspicious of strangers, throwing the basket of fruit Hela had brought straight back at her. Hela did not take kindly to people who did not accept her gifts with gratitude or repay her in compliments. Yet, the two women had formed an odd kind of friendship. It bloomed and wilted with the seasons.

Carissa wasn't sure what season it was for their friendship currently. So, she tried nonchalantly to draw a less partial picture of events.

"What room did Tabitha want?"

"That's the funniest part. Tabitha had a room on top deck like the rest of us, but no, she wanted a lower deck, for goodness knows what reason. I even told her the upper decks were much better, though you'd never know it with this dreadful rain."

"Did she get the room she wanted?"

"I don't know. We left. Fen said it was none of our business."

"Hela, darling, it was not our business," Fen chided lightly.

Hela picked up her butter knife and scraped butter onto her roll with just enough force to show annoyance. "I was only trying to help as a friend."

Carissa smirked ever-so-subtly. Hela used friendship as an excuse to "help" in everyone's business. It was a lovable flaw as long as Hela wasn't prying into one's own business. Then again, even Carissa wasn't above getting involved in others' affairs, if she felt there was something mysterious at work. She excused herself from the table, hugged Hela with the usual friendliness the elf expected, and promised to stop by her cabin later to see how she'd redecorated it into a "livable space."

Chaos, Hiya, and Cynth, stuffed to their capacity, flapped their sluggish wings and plopped themselves onto her shoulders. With their bellies full, Hiya and Cynth pushed one another for more room until Hiya decided enough was enough and drifted to Cameron's shoulder. Cynth did not hesitate to take his spot.

Cameron had stood, shared a firm handshake with Fen, and pushed in his chair by the time Hiya landed at the crook of his neck. Hiya clutched Cameron's ear with one hand and tugged, as if commanding him to move.

Cameron's eyes slid to his left shoulder. Hiya let go of the ear and waved an innocent hello. Shaking his head, Cameron followed Carissa out of the banquet hall.

"You're going to see Tabitha?" he asked.

"I just want to see if she's all right."

"That is unusual, wanting the lower decks, isn't it?"

"I can't think of a single reason why she'd want to be put in any of the lower cabins," Carissa said honestly.

Cameron shrugged. "She's always been unconventional."

That was true, but Tabitha was also smart. So was Otto. On top of that, they seemed to share Carissa's suspicion of Beathan. Though, unlike Carissa's assumption that something was off about her, Otto might have proof of her nefarious intentions.

On deck, the weather had only become foggier. With this low visibility, Carissa wondered if she'd even be able to find her own cabin, much less Tabitha's. The promenade was clear enough for her to see a few crewmen.

Tapping the nearest one on the shoulder, she said, "Excuse me."

The crewman turned. He was solemn and dreadfully severe, more like the druids Carissa imagined she'd see.

"I'm looking for the changeling Tabitha's room. Could you tell me where it is?"

"Switched to the lower quarters. Third deck, Room 13," one of the other crewmen answered.

"Thank you," Carissa and Cameron said simultaneously.

Cameron whistled. "Thirteen. That's unlucky. Or it is lucky to the fae? Or maybe to Tabitha? I never know what to expect with her."

Neither did Carissa. They found a staircase on the starboard side and descended. Two flights later, they made it to what looked like the crewmen's quarters. Though still pristine and shining, the lower decks, by their metallic nature, seemed ominous and cold. All the way at the stern side, they came upon Room 13.

Carissa knocked twice.

"Coming!" The steel door could not muffle the energy in Tabitha's voice.

"Sounds like she's over her anger," Cameron noted.

"She did get the room," Carissa whispered.

The door opened, but instead of the wide grin Carissa was expecting, the sullen frown of Mr. Otto Crimbal greeted her. He nodded and stepped back to let them inside.

Clothes flew everywhere, piling on top of the dresser, the lamp, the bedposts, and Tabitha herself. Bent over one of three open suitcases on the floor, Tabitha continued flinging one garment after another in search of something. Upon seeing Carissa, she jumped up. A multi-colored scarf caught on Tabitha in the process and draped itself over her right shoulder.

The bright colors attracted two of the nature faeries, who lifted it off of her and high into the air to fight over it. Chaos sat cross-armed where she was, simultaneously raising her head as if she was above such silly actions and glaring as if she were jealous she was missing the fun. It was just as well since Hiya and Cynth both wanted to wrap themselves in the garment. They tugged at each end of it until they broke into yet another brawl. Tabitha, ignoring the faerie fight inches from her nose, grinned and grabbed both of Carissa's hands.

"Come and see this sight. Isn't it beautiful?" She pulled her to the porthole window, this one was closer to ocean-level and, from there, Carissa could see the water fae accompanying the boat.

Shimmering, flat tails splashed in unison as they hit the water. Then up again came these seal-like creatures. Carissa gasped and Cameron whistled.

"Amazing," he said.

"A lot of noise." Otto shuffled over to the bed and grimaced as it squeaked beneath his weight.

Tabitha shook her head. "I didn't ask you to come, and I think it is breathtaking. There are kelpies at the front and these selkies here in the back. Oh, it's just wonderful!"

Chaos, meanwhile, had found an even more wondrous sight. She waved her hands to get Carissa's attention. Both she and Cameron gaped at a diamond ring and a band sitting on the dresser.

"The water fae are something, but so is this." Carissa pointed to the rings and looked between Otto and Tabitha. "Are you two engaged?"

"Married," Tabitha said, and she continued her search of whatever she was looking for in the room.

"Married?" Carissa and Cameron exclaimed in unison.

Carissa said, "Why didn't you tell us?"

"I just did." Tabitha blinked from where she sat on the floor.

"She means why didn't we know before? We would have loved to have seen the wedding," Cameron said.

Tabitha twisted to look at Otto. "I told you weddings have guests!"

"Not ones at city hall, my dear," Otto said, too engrossed in his book to be paying full attention to anything else.

It seemed that Tabitha's limited experience with social interaction and Otto's avoidance of people had resulted in this complete and utter surprise. Carissa knew Otto loved her, but she couldn't help but feel sorry for Tabitha for not having shared such a special day with her friends.

"Congratulations. We'll throw a big party for you and Otto when we get home," Carissa said awkwardly, reaching down for a hug.

"Thank you, I'd love that!" Tabitha reciprocated the embrace from where she sat.

Otto frowned at the thought of a party, but he sat up as Cameron made his way toward him to shake his hand and say his congratulations.

"Thank you. You're both very thoughtful," Otto said politely, but then he resumed his reading as if the whole affair were nothing to go on about. He flipped through pages of his ancient-looking book, scrutinizing each word as if there were no one in the room to whom he needed to pay any mind. Tabitha resumed her wild search, flinging items about without an intended target. Hiya and Cynth dropped the scarf to catch the next garment Tabitha tossed and the next one after that.

Carissa looked at Cameron, but he held his palms up confusedly. Chaos swooped over Tabitha's suitcase like a curious crow. Cameron walked forward, watching Tabitha's quixotic search with interest.

"So, what are you looking for?" he asked.

Tabitha stopped and looked up. "Looking for?"

"You're taking things out of your suitcase in a hurry." Carissa raised a blouse from the couch to illustrate her point.

"I'm unpacking." Tabitha's tone suggested she had no idea that her methods were…unique.

Chaos, hearing there was no treasure to find, lost interest in the suitcase and flew over to Otto's book.

"She couldn't keep a tidy space to save her life." Otto did not look up from his book except to swat the nature faerie away several times.

"Then you unpack." The cardigan Tabitha threw fell short of hitting Otto's leg.

Otto flipped a page. "After you, love."

Cameron stifled a laugh, not well enough. Tabitha's ears perked, and she tilted her chin up to look at him curiously. Carissa spoke up to cover the awkwardness.

"Tabitha, why did you want a room on the crewmen's deck?"

Tabitha paused. After a few seconds of fiddling with a dress, she said, "Sea sickness. The lower decks are better for that."

As nonchalant as she tried to sound, Tabitha appeared to be making up the excuse right then and there. Her nervousness manifested into more clothes throwing and then an abrupt stop to play with her hair. She stood.

"Um, I have a lot of unpacking to do, so we'll have to talk later." Tabitha stepped closer to the door, pushing Carissa backward.

She shooed the sprites gently with her palm. Carissa and Cameron had no choice but to say goodbye and start their way back up the stairs. Chaos, Hiya, and Cynth followed in the air behind them.

"Well, that was odd—and not just Tabitha-odd," Cameron said.

"The secret wedding or Tabitha's strange behavior?"

"When is Tabitha's behavior not strange? No, I meant the wedding. Do you think Hela knows?"

Carissa chortled. "If she knew, there wouldn't be a passenger on board this ship who didn't know it too. But that's not what I think is odd. Tabitha was definitely hiding something—not the wedding, but something about why they took that cabin. I don't think it's just sea sickness."

"Sea sickness," Cameron mused. "Wait, you don't think she's…?"

"No."

Carissa didn't want to divulge such an intimate secret, but she knew for a fact that Otto, by way of being a crimble, had been made of enchanted clay. Since a crimble changeling like Otto was birthed by magic and not born, he was incapable of giving life himself. Tabitha could not have a child as long as she was with Otto—at least, not without magical intervention.

"It has to be something else," she said.

"But what? The selkies?" Cameron asked.

Or Beathan? Carissa thought. She didn't want to even whisper the suggestion as long as they were nearing the upper deck. If there was a reason to suspect the water fae woman, there was no need to alert her to the fact that anyone suspected her.

As they set foot on the promenade again, Logan's booming voice called out, "Cam, Carissa, I'm glad I found you here. I've got a crewman who is very curious about Moss Hill. He would love to speak to a Mossie in more detail."

Cameron raised an eyebrow to Carissa. The sprites also cornered her with wide eyes and hands clasped together. Chaos didn't make a plea one way or another but looked between the captain, Cameron, and Carissa as if deciding what to do.

Carissa gave up. "You go, and you, too," she nodded at the sprites. Then, she raised her voice so Logan could hear her, "I'll meet you at the dinner tonight."

"Aye, 19:00 sharp," Logan replied.

Cameron kissed her on the cheek. "That's 7:00 p.m. at the captain's table."

"I know," she lied. She might have remembered something Raven said about the 24-hour timescale and dinner propriety, but she was too overwhelmed to recall it clearly. It was only the first few hours into the trip, and already it was stressing her out. It was a good thing she'd have a few hours to herself even without the sprites. Except for Chaos, who would likely make her practice what she was going to say to the Tuatha de Danann on their arrival in Hy Brasil.

She wished Raven had just told her what to say, instead of insisting the words needed to come from Carissa's heart. If only it weren't beating so loudly every time she thought about her mission. Maybe then she could hear what it was trying to say.

***

"'AND THIS IS our opportunity to create a better world for all of us. All we have to do is seize the chance.' What do you think?"

Chaos gave a thumbs down from her perch in the porthole. She'd spent just as much time enjoying how large her shadow was growing on the opposite wall as she had listening to Carissa's speech. Even now, her thumbs down became a bunny rabbit shadow puppet as Chaos moved her fingers against the setting sun. Carissa shook her head, trying to ignore the distraction. She bit her lip and twirled the pencil between her fingers. Staring at the notepad only made the words blur.

"I need a break." Carissa threw the speech onto the bed. Chaos floated toward the door. The clock above the dresser read 6:30 p.m., just enough time to get some fresh air before joining Cam and Logan for dinner. At least the clouds had cleared, so the night would be perfect for walking on the promenade.

Before she turned to leave, Carissa spied a shadow on the wall where Chaos's shadow puppets had been. It looked like the face of a person, pressing their cheek against the window to listen in. Carissa snapped her head toward the source. The porthole window was empty but wet. And there appeared to be mud on the glass. Carissa turned to face the door. Chaos was turning the lock open with her faerie dust.

Carissa grabbed the knob before Chaos could turn that, too. There was someone outside, she wanted to say. But, so what if there was? This was a ship, a fae ship, so any fae could be on deck for any reason. It might even be a crewman cleaning. Why was she so jumpy?

She talked herself out of it, turning the handle. Chaos tilted her head curiously at Carissa, then brushed it off as the cool night air flowed into the cabin. The two ventured out into the dusk.

Without realizing that she'd been holding her breath, Carissa let out a sigh of relief when she saw that there was no one outside. She became just as upset a second later when she realized that she'd almost stepped in a pile of mud resting just outside her door. She nearly twisted an ankle trying to avoid it. Still, some of it ended up on the tip of her shoe.

"For all the cleaning they do on this ship, they've missed this enormous mess. What is this?"

Carissa hesitated to inspect the strange substance. It looked like mud, but the pungent smell made her worry it was something left by a large animal. There were no large animals aboard that she knew of, and it didn't smell like fertilizer that had spilled from a bag. The aroma was…burnt.

The consistency was off, too. It lacked the graininess of mud, more like—

Carissa snapped to full height as she heard clanging sounds coming from the promenade. There was a yell, then more of the clash of metal on metal.

"Someone's fighting," Carissa told Chaos.

The two dashed across the deck, making it to the promenade just in time to see the swords swinging in action. Logan thrust his weapon at Cameron, who, thankfully, parried inches from his head. Logan laughed.

"You're getting the hang of it. You're not bad, actually. Light on your feet."

"Thanks, I've had practice using my feet for running." Cameron's self-deprecating remark was met with more laughter from Logan and his crewmen.

"Now you'll have practice using your arms for fighting."

They weren't the only ones practicing sword fighting. Hiya and Cynth's pretend battle kept going in the air above the crewmen's heads even after Cameron and Logan had stopped.

Carissa crossed her arms. Cameron caught sight of her eyes narrowing in on him. He handed the sword off to one of the observers, and Logan turned around.

"Ah, Cari, would you like to try your hand with a blade?"

"No, thank you," she said curtly.

If she'd been worried about Cameron drinking on deck and plummeting into the sea, she was now anxious about him taking a sword to the chest and stumbling overboard. Her worry made her remember Cameron's anger. She searched his face as her own expression softened. She couldn't read him because he wouldn't look her in the eye.

Cameron said, "I think I should wash up for dinner. Excuse me."

He swerved around Logan and past Carissa. She traced his footsteps. It was no good hoping he wasn't angry about the stern look she'd given him. He was walking too fast for her to apologize.

She tried anyway, but before she could speak, he stopped and turned around sharply, grabbing her by the shoulders and pulling her against a wall. Her eyes widened.

"Cam—"

He put a finger to her lips. The light at the end of the walkway flickered. A second later, something splashed into the water. Cameron released her.

"What did you see?" Carissa asked.

"I thought I—no, it couldn't be…"

Carissa rolled her eyes. *Could he say it any more cryptically?*

"Couldn't be what?"

He looked at her as if he'd seen a ghost. "What would Warren be doing on this ship?"

Scratch that, Carissa thought. It wasn't a ghost. He'd just seen the Ocean Reaper.

"But he was on a ship to Tir-Na-Nog. Raven was making sure of that. How could he be here?"

"Hi, guys!"

Carissa and Cameron both jumped. They spun around, ready to attack. Even Chaos readied a ball of faerie dust in her hands. It poofed out of existence when the owner of the voice stepped under the nearest light.

"Tabitha?" Carissa asked.

She was dressed in a puffy yellow and blue dress that looked like it had been made in the 1800s. It might have been collecting dust in a moth-filled closet for at least two hundred years. She swirled to show it off.

Cameron and Carissa coughed despite their best efforts. Tabitha, thankfully, didn't notice the dust. Smiling, she looked as radiant as her dress was faded.

"Hela said it was a formal dinner party."

Of course, Hela did. Every dinner was a formal one for Hela. Carissa smiled politely, and Cameron managed a weak compliment. Though, saying "nice dress" meant the opposite when accompanied by wincing.

The compliment was taken sincerely with a "thank you."

Carissa was thankful for Tabitha's obliviousness to Cam's faux pas. She also noticed that Tabitha was alone.

"Where's Otto?" Carissa asked.

"That's what I was going to ask you. I can't find him anywhere. I just asked all the crewmen, but they haven't seen him either." Tabitha scratched her head.

Like an anchor sinking to the ocean floor, Carissa's thoughts went to a dark, deep place. She almost struggled to breathe as she felt the full weight of her realization. The discovery she'd nearly made a few moments ago in front of her door was not a pile of mud.

It was clay.

If a crimble died, there would be no body. Only the clay from which the changeling was made would remain. The mud outside was all that was left of Otto Crimbal.

Chapter 6

Ripple Effect

Tabitha's voice shook as she tried to keep calm, "I can c-contact Raven. Her crows are f-flying around the ship. She said to s-s-send a letter if I need her." She sobbed at the end of her sentence.

Carissa rubbed her back while they sat on the edge of Tabitha's bed. She had refused to believe Carissa at first, but after alerting the captain and personally searching the whole upper deck and her quarters, she finally lost her resolve to ignore reality. Instead of breaking down like Carissa had expected, Tabitha dumped the flowers out of the vase in her bathroom and plunged the vessel into Cameron's hands. She asked him to gather up the clay that had previously been her husband. Then she sat on the bed, hugging her legs to her chest.

Carissa stayed with Tabitha while Cameron went to ask the captain if he'd found out anything. He'd been gone just a few minutes when the door swung open with a bang that caused Tabitha to let go of her legs, but she sulked after realizing it was Hela.

"Oh, you poor dear!"

She wrapped her arms around Tabitha and rocked her back and forth like an infant. With Hela's lacy blue dress taking up half the bed, Carissa thought it better to stand. Sal timidly stepped through the doorway at the same moment, wearing a bright yellow raincoat and lugging a basket of what appeared to be all the leftover cornucopias from the day's brunch. Carissa guided him to the dresser where he set the heap down.

Sal removed his hood and turned his watery eyes to Tabitha. "I'm so very sorry for your loss."

Tabitha struggled against her tears and Hela's grip. She patted Hela's arm several times before the elf let go. Then she straightened and nodded at Sal.

"Thank you, but I'll never forgive myself."

"For what?" Carissa asked.

Hela began fiddling with Tabitha's messy hair. "She means for Otto's death, but it's not your fault, Tabby. Who knows what really happened?"

Sal fiddled with his fingers. Then, spying the clothes that had now migrated to one big heap on the couch, he walked over and began folding. Carissa noted his jitteriness and wondered why Sal was taking Otto's death so hard. Sal was a compassionate person, but he didn't know Otto well, did he? And a few hours on a ship doesn't give much time for bonding.

Tabitha started sobbing. Hela rubbed her back as Tabitha gulped and drew in a deep breath. Her voice was thick and heavy. "I don't mean Otto's death. I'm sorry because the last thing I said to him was that I didn't want him here."

Carissa understood that. "You wanted to protect him," she said.

Tabitha's eyes nearly crossed in confusion. "What? I had no idea he was going to be in danger. No, I was angry because I told him I wouldn't have time to spend with him on this trip and he said it was fine because he came here as an attorney and not for me."

Hela gasped. "What a thing to say! That man does not have a single romantic bone in his body...did not. Oh, I apologize. One should never speak ill of the dead."

"May the reaper rest his soul," Sal's voice cracked. Then his eyes widened. "I don't mean the Ocean Reaper—not the last one anyway. Have they got a new reaper? Oh, I hope someone has claimed his soul. Someone good, I mean."

Carissa put a hand on Sal's shoulder. She would have said something to console him, but she wasn't even sure Otto had a soul. Was it only magic that brought a crimble to life? Or had there been more to him than that?

Tabitha stood, grabbed a notepad by the bedside, and began scribbling furiously. When she was done, she ripped the paper harshly enough for Hela to utter an "oh my." Then she shouted, "Chaos! Chaos!"

"She's with Cameron," Carissa said. "Why?"

"I need her to fly up to the top of the mast and give this to one of the crows."

"Fly up to the...there's a terrible fog. The poor faerie will catch a cold," Hela said.

"A cold? Otto is dead!"

Hela stood and wrapped an arm around Tabitha. "I know you're scared—"

"I'm not scared. I'm furious, and I'm going to catch the killer."

"Killer? How do you know he was killed?" Sal went whiter than a ghost.

"From where he was found, he couldn't have fallen. And crimbles don't have heart attacks. It looks like he just dissolved," Carissa explained.

"By magic," Tabitha added.

Carissa heard the footsteps in the hall from the open doorway. She stepped forward. Reaching a hand out to take Tabitha's letter, she said, "I'm sure Chaos will agree to take this right away."

Tabitha handed the letter over.

"I still think—"

Hela was interrupted by Fen and Cameron entering the cabin. The three faeries all swirled over Tabitha's head. Faerie dust rained down their healing blessings over her. She embraced the sprites.

Cameron walked to Carissa and wrapped an arm around her. "The whole ship has been cleared. There's no one but the crew aboard. If Otto was attacked, there's no sign."

"But you saw the Ocean Reaper," Tabitha said.

Cameron rubbed the back of his neck. "I thought I did— maybe. It was too dark for me to be sure."

"So, what is Logan going to do now?" Carissa asked.

"He's increased speed to get to Rhys Dwfen by morning. We will stop there until we get some answers about what happened," Fen explained.

Hela looked at Sal. "And you can see your birthplace and find out more about your parents."

Sal looked down and mumbled, "Doesn't seem as important now."

"Nonsense, two things can be important at once. We'll solve Otto's case and pay respects to your parents all at the same time. Trust me."

Hela reached out to squeeze both Tabitha's and Sal's arms at once. The confidence in her voice reminded Carissa of a mother's gentle assurances. She smiled to see Hela so well prepared for her parental role. Fen bowed his head to Tabitha, then took Hela's hand and escorted her out of the room.

Sal bowed, too. "I'm so, so sorry for your loss." He turned quickly, but Carissa caught sight of a tear leaving his cheek.

"Why don't you come up and have dinner with us?" Carissa suggested to Tabitha.

"I'm all right. I've got plenty." She pointed to the basket Sal had brought.

Hiya and Cynth took that as an invitation to unwrap it. Chaos left Tabitha's shoulder to wander about the room.

Carissa followed her with her eyes until she disappeared under the bed. She raised an eyebrow at the sprite but decided that whatever Chaos was doing, she'd be fine for a few minutes.

Cameron looked from the fruit basket to Tabitha. "Do you mind if we stay and share it with you?"

"Yes," she snapped. Then she put a hand to her head. "No, that was rude of me, but how do I say it? I'd like some time to myself without people, is that rude?"

"It's not rude at all." Carissa left Cam's side to hug Tabitha. "We're in Cabin 4 upstairs if you need us."

Tabitha nodded. "And don't forget about that letter!" she called out as they left.

Carissa waved it in the air. "Hiya, Cynth, put those oranges down. Chaos, let's go!"

Cynth was the first to listen, so Carissa handed the letter to her.

Cynth held both hands out wide as Carissa instructed the sprites, "The three of you take this up to the mast. Make sure the crows have it before you let go."

Tabitha's face visibly relaxed as the faeries raced past Carissa in a blur. With them gone, Carissa stepped out of the room and walked with determination toward the upper deck.

"Where are you going so fast?" Cameron hurried behind, with little time to properly shut the door.

"Sal was hiding something," Carissa said.

Cameron caught up with her so that she could see the quizzical expression on his face. "Sal? Why would he hide anything from us?"

On the last step, Carissa spied a tall, yellow raincoat. There was no rain yet, but the fog had thickened to the point where Carissa could only see the coat because of its bright, color. He paced along the starboard walkway, occasionally stopping to peer over the ship's railing. Carissa shot a glance at Cameron.

"Sal?" he called out.

The hooded coat moved close enough for Carissa to see the owner's face. Wide eyes welled beneath the yellow hoodie. Sal wiped a tear and sniffled.

"What is going on?" Carissa asked.

Cameron added for good measure, "You know something about Otto's death, don't you?"

Sal broke into sobs. Carissa reached her arm out and she and Cameron led him to their cabin where he could sit on the sofa. Carissa sat with him while Cameron dragged a chair over.

When he was finally composed enough to speak, he took pauses to steady his flow of tears.

"It's my fault. Otto came to me two days ago about an account he had from my relatives in Rhys Dwfen, cousins, I think. Fudge said my parents had money and things left to me in their will. He's been working with Otto to get them back for me, but my cousins said they won't release the money until someone investigates my parents' death."

Otto was an accountant, but Carissa had no idea that he'd been communicating with anyone outside of Moss Hill. She wondered if Tabitha knew his real reasons for joining them on this voyage. But his real reason hit Carissa like a rogue wave.

"Investigate? It was an accident, wasn't it?"

"Yes, Otto said it was just an excuse for them to keep my parents' wealth, but he must've gotten some new evidence because yesterday he said he came with us to investigate their claims. He thinks they were murdered!"

Sal's sobs shook his whole body. Carissa put an arm around him.

Cameron gently patted his shoulder. "I don't think his death had anything to do with your parents. You know this trip we're on isn't just a cruise."

"But that's what worries me. Otto was snooping around this ship. He even stole a book from the captain's library."

"Which book?" Carissa asked.

Sal shrugged. "I don't know."

"Am I missing something?" Cameron asked. "Why would he snoop around here?"

"Because the *Scuabtuinne* has been sailing this area for hundreds of years. It was a ship crashing that killed my parents: a ghostlike ship that, as suddenly as it crashed, was swept back into the water by a huge wave and sank. If anyone knew anything about a ship like that, it would be the *Scuabtuinne* crew."

"It might even be the *Scuabtuinne*," Carissa realized.

The *Scuabtuinne* was an enchanted ship with the ability to split the waves as well as sink beneath them. Ghostlike could be a descriptor, as it also had the ability to switch between the human and Otherworld as easily as a single fae.

Cameron shook his head. "I don't know. I don't see Logan crashing a ship, or fleeing the scene of a crime."

Carissa put a hand to her forehead. His hero worship of the captain was triggering a headache. Cameron had only met Captain Logan days ago, and today he was sword fighting. Logan certainly had an effect on people.

Sal took out a handkerchief and blew his nose. "All I know is, he was helping me investigate, and now he's dead."

Carissa rubbed Sal's back in small, comforting circles with her palm. Not knowing what to say, she looked at Cameron.

"It'll be okay, Sal. We'll get to the bottom of this," Cameron said.

Carissa squeezed Sal's shoulder. "We'll help you find out who did this, I promise."

***

THE NATURE FAERIES did not return by the time Sal had left. For one terrifying second, Carissa imagined all sorts of horrors that could have happened to them. Then, a knock on the porthole window caught her attention. Three shivering faeries appeared in the fog.

Carissa's heart thudded with every footstep. She thrust open the door. A gust of wind helped her along.

The faeries entered. Cameron helped Carissa pull the door shut while Hiya and Cynth rushed onto the bed and under the covers. Chaos circled Carissa as if celebrating, apparently not as cold as the others.

"Where have you three been?"

Chaos pointed downward while the two nature faeries pointed up. The up Carissa understood. Hiya and Cynth had taken the letter to the mast. Poor things. It shouldn't have taken them so long, but she also should have noticed the length of time.

She guessed why Chaos was pointing down.

"Were you in Tabitha's room all this time?"

Chaos nodded, suspiciously holding her hands out in front of her as if carrying something substantial. Carissa raised an eyebrow.

"What is in your hands?" Carissa asked.

Chaos closed her eyes. Her wings fluttered, and the sprites gathered around her. Holding their own hands up, they used their faerie dust to work some kind of spell together. Out of thin air—or the Otherworld, Carissa assumed—a blue, faded book appeared in her hands. Smiling, she held it up for Carissa to read.

Cameron lifted the book and held it between them.

"*The Riches of Rhys Dwfen?*" he read the title aloud.

Carissa took the spine, recognizing the lettering. "It's the book Otto Crimbal was reading. You took this from Tabitha's room?"

Looking very pleased with herself, Chaos slid her hands behind her back and a grin stretched across her face. Carissa should have chided Chaos for thievery, but she felt a glimmer of hope in today's gloom. This clue might lead to answers about Otto's death.

Cameron peered over Carissa's shoulder as she flipped through the pages. "Could Otto have been after Sal's inheritance?"

Carissa walked to the desk. Cameron took the chair next to Carissa, and the sprites sat cross-legged beside the book. She flipped to page one. "You're missing a bigger question: Why does Logan have a book like this in the first place?"

"It's a ship, they travel," Cameron said, adding, "all right, let's say there's something strange in Logan having the book—how does that connect the *Scuabtuinne* to the death of Sal's parents?"

Carissa's eyes turned to the book. "That might be the very question Otto Crimbal was trying to answer."

Chapter 7

No Safe Harbor

Carissa awoke to the sound of a horn blasting. Her eyes fluttered open and shut a few times before she was able to look out the window. The fog had not lifted. Her head felt as cloudy, and her muscles ached.

She groaned along with the noise her stomach was making. Captain Logan had sent room service to all the rooms last night, but she hardly felt like eating after the formal dinner had been canceled in light of last night's murder.

Murder.

Carissa put a hand to her forehead. She was already thinking of Otto's death like an investigator. Conspiracy theories had cluttered her thoughts up until she'd fallen asleep and were returning to her now.

A long night of reading meant a headache this morning. It wouldn't have been any better if she'd turned in when Cameron had called it a night for himself. She would have just tossed and turned, partly from the unsteady swaying of the ship in stormy seas and partly from worry. The book had been full of Rhys Dwfen legends and artifacts. Many of them would be a motive for murder if Otto had those treasures. Since he didn't own any of them, to Carissa's knowledge, she couldn't figure out how Otto's interest in Rhys Dwfen treasures connected to his death—if it had a connection at all.

Carissa kept circling around the possibilities.

Had Logan killed Otto to hide the *Scuabtuinne's* involvement in Sal's parents' death? Had Otto caught Beathan, Gerard, or one of the water fae conspiring with Niall Shae? Was he, Warren, or some third-party stowaway aboard that Otto had stumbled upon—to his misfortune?

The ship's horn blasted again—five times in short succession. Carissa sat up. Horn blasts meant one thing: they had arrived on the island of Rhys Dwfen.

Carissa patted the pillow next to her. "Hiya, Cynth, Chaos, come on, get up. We're here."

Tiny eyes opened and closed. Hiya rolled over. Chaos sat up, scratched her head, and pulled the covers off of her little fae friends. Hiya and Cynth followed her lead, but much slower and more begrudgingly.

Cameron, already up and apparently outside, knocked on the cabin's front entrance instead of his door to the adjoining room.

"One second," Carissa called out, quickly changing while the sprites "showered" under the bathroom sink.

She pulled on a short-sleeve red blouse and jean capris. Then, Carissa opened the door. Cameron came in wearing a white shirt with a navy anchor on the right pocket and dark blue pants that made it look like he was ready for sailing. It wasn't the exact same outfit as the other sailors, but it was as close as his closet offered.

Ignoring that, Carissa gave him a peck on the cheek and asked, "How late am I? Is everyone ready for shore?"

Cameron held his arms around her a moment longer. "Sal's already waiting at the top of the gangway. He's been pacing out there since breakfast was served. He says he's too nervous to eat. There's still a bunch of fruit out if you want some, but Logan says the market ashore offers plenty if you want to wait."

Carissa's stomach protested with another groan, but she said, "I'll wait."

She brushed her teeth as Chaos blow-dried Cynth and Hiya with her faerie dust magic. The sprites came out radiantly ready to go.

As Cameron waited, he updated her on what Logan had found. "Logan said it's a good thing you wanted to stop here. The fog was too harsh to keep traveling through. The day doesn't look much better. The fog made it hard to search the top deck, but there's no sign of an intruder on any of the lower decks anyway.

"What about the water fae?"

"What about them?"

"They're surrounding the boat. Any one of them might have climbed aboard and harmed Otto."

"Well, if they did, Fen will find out today." Cameron said. "He's staying behind with Logan to start interviews with the crewmen. I'm sure the water fae will be a part of that. But what makes you think they were involved and not just any of the crewmates?"

"They go on and off the ship, and there was water right beside Otto's...remains." The word "body" wasn't quite right, but neither was "clay." Otto had been more than that to many people, Tabitha most of all. Carissa threw on her pink raincoat and continued, "Have you seen Tabitha? How is she?"

Cameron opened the door. "Hela's with her. She's refusing to come with us to shore. Logan is a little worried she and Hela might interfere with investigations, but they've been staying in Tabitha's room so far this morning."

The nature faeries followed Carissa and Cameron through the promenade. The deck was filled with druids in their white uniforms, but Carissa saw them through a darker lens now. Each was a suspect in Otto's murder. But none were as suspicious as the absent water fae. With the ship at rest, could any one of them have simply disappeared into the sea? Had the murderer already swum away?

Sal paced right where Cameron said he'd been waiting. The nature faeries covered him in comforting hugs. He smiled and released them so they could settle back in Carissa's purse.

"Is it just the three of us? No druids coming along?" Carissa said.

Sal stretched a hand toward the green landmass behind him. "Rhys Dwfen is supposed to be——"

"The friendliest port in the world," Carissa recalled his statement. "All right, then what are we waiting for? Let's find your answers, Sal."

***

"THE ISLAND OF the Deep Rhys, or Rhys Dwfen, was named after a flower," Sal said as they stepped out of the fog. The cloudiness hung over the sea, but it hadn't even come close to touching the land.

Though he'd been a baby when he'd last seen this island, Sal explained that his uncle, Fudge, had told him about the beauty of the island. Words fell short of the place.

They passed by a few feet of sand until the dock took them straight into a field of flowers and shrubbery. Carissa had never seen such greenery so close to shore. The pier split off into two paths. On their left, picnics were laid out for families of elfkins, or rhys dwfen, as they were really known.

To the right, the pier led to rows and rows of booths overflowing with people of all ages and faerie backgrounds. Sweet and savory scents blended in the air—from peppery spices to pickled herring to berry pies to faerie butters. The sound of ringing bells and merchants calling out their items to potential customers competed for Carissa's attention.

"Have a try of this iced orchid tea, miss."

Carissa held a hand up to say no, though the refreshments did look good, the day was not so hot that she needed anything so cold.

The lady in charge of the next booth noted Carissa's interest in the handbags laid out on the table. She picked up one of the small change purses.

"Genuine spider silk from a Darwin's bark spider. The silk is imported from Madagascar, but the purse itself is made here. No one's breaking into this—that's a guarantee."

Carissa couldn't help but stare at the red change purse in the woman's hands. What looked like genuine flower petals were embroidered right into the fabric, glowing at the edges. It mesmerized her.

"How much?"

"What would you like to trade?"

Right. Sal had explained that, too. He had brought several items from Moss Hill with which to make trades, but Carissa, who hadn't even planned to stop here, had not.

"I could give her this," Sal fumbled through his duffel bag, but Carissa gripped his wrist gently.

"That's okay," she said.

"I'd take money, too," the woman said.

Carissa shook her head. She smiled guiltily at the woman to whom she'd given false hope of a sale and moved on.

With plenty of shoppers in the market, however, she didn't seem the least bit bothered. Carissa had a few items in her purse with which she was willing to part, but only for that heavenly lemon and blueberry scent tickling her nose from somewhere ahead.

"Excuse me," Sal took out a picture painting of a male goblin and female rhys dwfen holding a baby. Holding it up for the woman to see, he said, "Do you know a Grem and Poppy who had a baby son named Sal about a hundred years ago?"

The woman shrugged. "Sorry, I'm only eighty. You'll have to ask someone older."

Sal folded the paper back up. "Thank you."

"I didn't know you had a picture," Carissa reached out before he'd put it away.

He set the plate in front of Carissa, blushing. "Drew it myself from Fudge's description."

The mother had the same smile as Sal. The father had the same pointed chin and dark eyes. Those features had always made Sal stand out from the elves in Moss Hill. He even stood out on this island, and so did his father in the picture.

"Forgive me, Sal, but you said your father was a goblin, wasn't he?"

"A goblin pirate was the rumor. All we know for sure is he was a duende, but that doesn't mean he was unseelie."

Carissa didn't know much about duende, except that they dwelled in rock caverns and murky places. They tended to be from the Americas, though they also resided on islands across the Pacific. If he'd come here, he was a long way from home. A pirate made sense. It would explain how he'd traveled the fae seas and ended up settling on Rhys Dwfen. To be fair, duende weren't necessarily unfriendly, unseelie faeries, but if the title "goblin" were accurate, then a pirate was about the only explanation that made sense. And if he'd been a pirate, then he may have made some enemies along the way.

"Come on, there's a lot of vendors to ask. We'd better keep going." Cameron started walking to the next booth.

"You two go ahead," Carissa insisted. "I'm going to get some breakfast. I'll catch up as soon as I'm done."

"Should I come with you?" Cameron asked.

"Not unless you want something other than cornbread, because I'm going to eat every last crumb they have," she said, pointing to the sign three booths ahead. It flapped in the wind just above the booth, reading: *Bailing's Baked Goods*. Cameron chuckled and agreed that they would meet at the end of the row in about twenty minutes.

Carissa made her way over. She wasn't really sure if cutting between booths was allowed, but no one made a fuss. A few merchants offered her their goods, but none pressed when she politely declined each one.

At Bailing's, a kind, gray-haired man with plump cheeks and a friendly smile said, "What can I get you, friend?"

Carissa pointed at the pastries her nature faeries were already circling. "What will you take for a piece of that lemon and blueberry cornbread?"

"That? It's no cornbread, love. That's a buttercream frosted berry lemon bread, and it's…" His eyes widened as they followed something behind Carissa. She turned to see what had caught his attention.

Sal and Cameron finished at the booth opposite them and nodded at Carissa as they passed by. Carissa glanced between them and the baker. He paled liked he'd seen a ghost.

"Do you recognize him?" Carissa asked.

"I, uh, no." He laughed. "I thought I did for a moment, but no, it couldn't have been him."

"Who?"

Baker Bailing cut a healthy slice of lemon bread while the nature faeries rubbed their hands together in anticipation.

"An old goblin who lived here. Caused much trouble said some folks, but that was just their fear talking."

"Why were they afraid?"

He stared at the bread a minute before grabbing the plate. "Suppose it doesn't matter now. He came in here looking for treasure, soon enough he was telling tall tales about talismans and curses."

"He was a pirate?"

"Some said. Not what he called himself, though."

"What did he call himself?"

"A sailor for one of the king's merchant ships."

"The King of Sidhe and Elves?"

"The very one. But he'd been stranded by a rogue wave—he and his crew, though there was not one crewmate to speak of. That's when people got the idea that he'd been a pirate thrown overboard by his own goblin captain."

"How do you know the captain was a goblin?"

The baker shrugged. "Had to be if it was a goblin pirate ship." He handed the plate to her and sighed. "I never believed it. He was far too nice for piracy. He even managed to marry the most sought after girl in town."

"Let me guess, she was beautiful, wealthy, and kind?" Carissa's guess was more her remembering how Sal had described her. It was nice to know that the description was shared by the town who knew her.

"Beautiful, wealthy, and kind, my dear, here all three are the same. Compassion is everything, and she had it in her more than most."

Now Carissa had to ask, knowing the sour-faced Fudge as well as she did, "Was her brother the same way?"

His eyes narrowed. Only then did she realize that she'd let herself get carried away. Bailing thought he was having a conversation with a complete stranger to the situation, but she'd just revealed that she knew the people involved.

She smiled.

"I'm a friend. That man you just saw is Sal, he's Grem and Poppy's—"

"Their son," Bailing's eyes teared.

"We're here to find out what we can about his parents' death."

His eyes searched down the row, but Sal was long gone. He breathed in and out softly, then wiped his eyes as he answered. "I don't know about that, only the rumors."

"Even that much might help."

"There was so much speculation, from pirates to the *Scuabtuinne* to the Reaper himself."

"The Reaper?"

"A wave swallowed them up—that's what some people said."

"Wasn't it a boat that crashed into shore?"

"There was damage to the beach. It looked like a boat had come into land."

"But no one saw the actual boat?"

"No. But there are boats that appear and disappear on our shores. We've seen it happen once or twice in each generation. None that crash, though. And none that take people's lives."

"Were there any witnesses?"

"Only Sal himself, but he was such a little thing. I don't think he'd remember."

Carissa pursed her lips. It hadn't struck her as strange until now that only Sal had been spared from the boat attack. Fudge had told him it was because he'd wandered off, but now that she knew that no one had actually seen the boat, she couldn't be sure that Sal's parents weren't attacked and he was spared because he was too young to speak as a witness. Or perhaps whoever it was just hadn't had the heart to kill a child.

Carissa looked out toward the *Scuabtuinne*, hoping it wasn't someone on that ship. But if there was a boat at sea, she couldn't see it. The fog was so heavy out past the marketplace that she could not even see the ocean.

"Is it always this foggy?" she asked.

"No, can't say it is, though come to think of it, it was that way the day Sal's parents died. And it rained that day, too, which it never does here. It's like the whole earth knew what had happened and was crying."

The earth wasn't the only one. Bailing's speech had moved the nature faeries to tears. The three sprites broke off pieces of lemon bread and shoveled them into their mouths as they sobbed over Sal's story. Bailing started to cut off another piece.

Carissa held a palm up. "Oh, I don't know if I have enough things of value to trade, all I have is…" She shuffled through her purse to find something she could use to pay.

Bailing handed her the slice anyway. "You gave me the good news that Sal is still alive. That's enough to barter with me for all the lemon bread in my kitchen."

Carissa smiled. "Thanks," she said, taking the offering.

The nature faeries, having had their fill, left the rest of the uneaten bread alone and flew above Carissa's head as she walked.

Part of Carissa wanted to wait to catch up with Cameron and Sal and possibly find a table and chair to sit at and savor the eating, but a far stronger impulse urged her to pick up the bread and take one mouth-watering bite.

"Mmm," she moaned in delight as the mixed berry flavor burst in her mouth.

She could have enjoyed another bite, if not for the stranger bumping into her shoulder. The lemon bread flew out of her hand. She watched it fall with heartbreak, but the laughter behind her was more unsettling. She twisted around to see a group of elves in rugged black and brown worn-out leather clothing.

"Watch where you're going," said the one in the middle. The elf had three sets of rings on his pointed ears, one in his nose, and a tattoo of a jellyfish across his cheek and neck. Carissa probably should have left this roguish elf alone, but she was angry and hungry and more than a little tired.

"You ran into me, so I suggest you take your own advice." She straightened her raincoat and walked away. She did stop to pick up the lemon bread and throw it into a trash bin, but it landed on the floor when the elf knocked into her again.

This time, she fell to the ground. The sprites took to the air, fists raised, faerie dust flying. Carissa held them back with a little elf-light forcefield that not only protected them but served as a warning to her attacker. She lit her other hand, too.

"Nature faeries and a fiery temper? That's not enough to fight with me."

Bailing, the baker, came out of his booth.

"No need to ruin a lovely day, gentlemen. How about a complimentary pastry?"

The elf smiled. "In a minute."

From Carissa's right came another voice and a hand to help her up. "Go now. And say thank you for the baker's offer," he warned the others.

The voice belonged to another elf who had the same type of clothes but kinder eyes. They shined a bright green. He ran a hand through his thick, red hair.

"Are you all right?" he asked.

"Yeah, all except for my lemon bread," she was finally able to lift it off the ground and throw it into the bin.

"Let me buy you another one." He led the way back to Bailing's booth.

The old man smiled uncomfortably as the goons surrounding his booth parted for them. The elf who had rescued Carissa opened a drawstring leather bag and lifted a handful of coins. They looked like pirates' booty, or at least the ancient type of treasure Carissa imagined sitting in a sunken pirate ship at the bottom of the sea.

"We take nothing free, got it?" he said to his crew, or what Carissa assumed was his crew.

They nodded as they chewed and swallowed their food. Bailing took the coins with a grin and handed Carissa her lemon bread. Carissa uttered her thanks, which the nature faeries repeated through nods.

"I've heard Rhys Dwfen has the friendliest shores. Even the villains are benevolent," Carissa said.

The elf laughed. "I must apologize, my friends are hot-tempered, but what they lack in manners they make up for in loyalty."

"And to whom are they loyal?" Carissa asked.

He bowed. "Neal."

Carissa gasped.

"Is something the matter?"

"Niall Shae?" She felt the words escape involuntarily.

"Why would an elf have a surname?" Neal put a hand to his chin.

Her heart raced for a moment and then eased up. This was not her cousin. Niall wasn't even an elf. Besides that, the names had a slight difference in pronunciation. *Nye-all* and *Neal* were two different things. The only connection was their similarity.

She laughed at herself. "Never mind, it's nothing. I'm Carissa." She extended a hand.

He took it the old-fashioned way and kissed it. Then, holding on a second longer, he said, "I am very pleased to meet you, Carissa. May I walk you to your destination?"

"No, thank you. I'm fine as long as I don't run into any more hot-tempered elves."

"If you do," he handed her a calling card, a magical means of contacting a fae, this one being a black card with the symbol of a sea snake on it. There was no visible writing, as only elf-light could activate it.

"Thank you." Carissa pocketed the card and hoped she would never have reason to use it.

Chapter 8

Washer Woman

At the end of the row of booths, an unpaved road twisted along a gravelly path. On an overcast morning like this one, the wind sang over the gray stones. The contrast between the empty trail and the festive marketplace around her made Carissa stop, raise an eyebrow, and search the crowd for her companions. It wasn't like Cameron to leave Carissa waiting. Yet here she was at the end of the first aisle with neither Cameron nor Sal in sight.

The last vendor, a grandmotherly-type whose candied yams might have been tempting if not for the growing pit in Carissa's stomach, responded negatively to her inquiry about them. "Wish I could help. An islander who looks half-goblin, you'd think I'd remember that. And a human? We don't really get those on our shores."

"Thank you anyway." Carissa turned her eyes to vendors on the opposite side.

"Uh, miss?" the rhys dwfen woman called her back. "My dear girl, I hate to ask with you all distressed like that, but…"

"What is it?" Carissa braced herself. The woman looked as distraught as she felt.

"Well, I don't mean to nitpick, but I will be needing a trade for the yam your wee little ones are nibbling at."

Carissa's eyes reached the table with dismay as the now bright-orange sprites licked their sticky fingers. Chaos, just as

74

guiltily orange as her friends, tried kicking Hiya and Cynth to get them to notice Carissa's scowl.

"Sorry about them." Carissa fished around for something worth the yam. She took out a change purse. "Will you take money?"

The woman took the coins offered to her with a chuckle. "No problem, dearie. Hope you find your friends."

A rise in the woman's voice might have gone unnoticed by all but elfish ears. Carissa thanked the woman and nodded for the nature faeries to take their piece of candied yam and follow. While Hiya and Cynth kept themselves distracted with an aerial tug-of-war over their sweet potato dessert, Chaos met Carissa's eyes with a look that told Carissa she, too, hadn't missed the fact that this woman was hiding something.

"I know," Carissa whispered, tapping her shoulder for Chaos to land on. "I can't just accuse her of lying, though. I'll have to find…"

Carissa's eyes settled on a book tent four shops back. *Raz's Rare Books and Artifacts,* read a wooden sign hanging from a light-blue canopy. White bookshelves held stacks of worn-out tomes. It was precisely the type of shop Cameron would have been tempted to browse—Sal or no Sal.

Beelining straight for the vendor, Carissa led the sprites inside the booth where glass cabinets showcased books so old they might've withered to dust in the open air. A white-haired, lean man of average height and build adjusted his bowtie and smoothed his royal blue velvet tailcoat. His otherwise unattractive face lit from the shine of his sapphire eyes beneath his glasses as he greeted them with a warm smile. Simultaneously, he laid a protective hand on the enormous telescope, which Hiya and Cynth were attempting to use to look out at the ocean.

"Can I help you?" the man asked.

"I hope so, um, Mr. Raz."

"Just Raz." He bowed, nudging himself between the sprites and the books.

"Did a human come here with a rhys dwfen?"

"You mean Sal?" The man picked up a rag to wipe the cabinets, despite the fact that the faeries had not actually touched them.

"That's right. Did you see which way he went?"

"Are you asking about Sal or the human?" The man walked around the table to the open shelves and began rearranging the artifacts.

"Did they split up?"

"Once they got to the road."

Carissa looked back as far down the row as she could. The road was not visible from here. But why would they have gone down the road in the first place? She couldn't think of a good reason why they wouldn't wait for her.

"Did either of them say which way they were going?"

"To see Grem and Poppy's grave, rest their souls."

"You knew them?" Carissa asked.

Raz took off his spectacles and tugged a purple cloth from his tailcoat pocket. Absorbed in the act of cleaning the frames, he said, "It was a long time ago and yesterday all at once. That's how memories work, don't they? The ones that matter." He put the glasses back on, his pointed ears twitching. "Books are like that too. I don't suppose you are interested in any of these?" He took a book and opened it carefully to the title page. "The stories here are far older than me, perhaps even older than this island. I've collected them from all over the world."

Carissa pulled the sprites away from the bookshelves with her palm. Now she understood why the bookseller was taking such good care of his merchandise. One glance at the date in the book confirmed it was a several centuries-old treasure.

"I was really just looking for my friends. So, Sal is seeing his parents' grave. Do you know where Cam, uh, the human, went?"

"I suppose the human was interested in the legend from that book." He pointed to a volume out in the open shelves with a red leather binding and a curve to the cover and spine.

Chaos read the cover before Carissa, who deciphered it aloud, "*Talismans of*...what is that word?"

Chaos made a waving motion with her hand. Carissa squinted. "Water? Waves? The ocean?"

Hiya and Cynth watched as if this were an intense moment in a theatrical performance. Chaos traced the first letter carefully, not touching the book under Raz's watchful eye.

"T? T...E..."

"Tethra, one of the Fomorians," Raz finished. "Bet you never heard of them. Most people haven't since the Tuatha de Danann sent them back into the sea. I told your friend the history. It's quite interesting, actually—"

"I'm sorry, but I really just need to know how this relates to where he went." Cameron could fill her in on the history when she found him, which she was hoping would be sooner rather than later. Since her encounter with the elves, she knew this island was not as danger-free as they'd thought.

"I imagine he went to see if the washer woman is on the road now."

"What washer woman?"

"The Fomorian. The phantom. She comes around this time of day and year. People tend to avoid the road because of her bad omens and all."

"Where on the road?"

"Oceanside, to the right. Left goes into town. I advised your friend to go left."

"He went right, and Sal went left?" Carissa stepped away from the booth and searched what she could see of the road.

Raz stepped to the booth's edge and nodded. "The grave is a better destination than the washer woman."

***

THE WASHER WOMAN wielded a wet cloth like a weapon. She gripped it tightly and seethed at Cameron. Her withered skin and clothes sagged on her small, aged body.

Her voice rasped, "Leave, or someone will die."

"I've heard you make threats, but also that you grant wishes. I caught sight of you, now you have to help me."

"Helping often hurts instead. Go away."

"Just one wish then: the Talisman of Tethra."

The washer woman stopped her washing. She hobbled toward Cameron. Carissa, watching from around the corner, lit her elf-light in her palms.

"The talisman was already wished for."

"By who?"

"Someone who knew more about me than the five minutes of knowledge you've acquired at the book shop. Forget the talisman. If you must ask, ask for something else."

"Fine, what about a way to protect ourselves against the unseelie on the seas."

Carissa could swear she saw the washer woman roll her eyes. She pulled at something on her neck. At least ten necklaces rattled as she sifted through them. Her wrinkled hand trembled while selecting one that resembled a clamshell.

Cameron took it in both hands. "What's this?"

"A talisman."

"But you said," Cameron stopped himself. "This isn't the Talisman of Tethra, is it?"

"This talisman will protect someone who needs it at a time when they are most vulnerable. The other will lead to the death of one as good as family."

Even from so far away, Carissa could see Cameron's jaw drop. "I don't understand, is the talisman cursed?"

"It may as well be—for the one who will die."

"Is that a threat?"

Carissa had heard enough. She crossed the bridge. Toward the end of the crossing, dizziness pulled at her. She thought for a second she might fall, but her next step brought her to solid ground. Cameron turned to face her, and the washer woman did not move.

Carissa caught her breath. "She's not threatening, she's predicting."

The washer woman finally faced her. Her eyes darkened as an ominous cloud passed over her features. She had seen something when she'd looked at Carissa.

"What do you see?" Carissa asked.

"You, treading between life and death."

"And can you also see the past?"

"The past is trickier. Future and past are not always what they seem, though only the future is seen as changeable."

"How can we see the far past?" Carissa asked.

Cameron answered, "A mirror! I read it in your grandfather's study—you can see the past with the help of the mirror...the mirror of…"

The old woman waved a hand. "There is no name for it. It's like these talismans, you only need an enchanted mirror."

"How do we make one?" Carissa asked.

"Better yet, do you have one?" Cameron added.

The washer woman limped to her bundle by the water's edge, which apparently held more than just clothes. Out of an empty bag, she pulled out a black, handheld mirror.

Carissa took it in her right hand. The faeries swirled around it. Carissa pulled it out of the way.

"Three is all you get, and it's not without a price."

"Three what?" Cameron inquired.

"What's the price?" Carissa asked in time with Cameron's question.

The washer woman held a shaky hand out to Hiya and gestured for him to hand over his sweet. Hiya looked between Cynth, Chaos, and Carissa, all of whom nodded toward the washer woman. Pouting, Hiya flew to her open palm and let go. The sticky food fell from his fingertips. She popped it into her mouth.

Carissa grimaced. She would not have eaten it so eagerly after it had passed between the three of them. The woman didn't seem to mind.

"Three wishes," she finally answered.

"But you only gave us two," Cameron countered.

"Three, unless you're choosing not to live? Because the sight of me means death unless I save you." The washer woman's bony finger pointed to the bridge, which was rickety and broken from this side. If they attempted to cross the river again, they'd drown!

"What happened to the bridge?"

"Broken for a week now. If I hadn't saved you on the crossing, you'd have lost your footing and drowned. If I don't save you going back, you'll also drown."

"I don't remember you saving me or Carissa." Cameron slid an arm around Carissa as if protecting her after the fact.

But Carissa remembered the sick and dizzy feeling she had on the crossing. She'd only felt that way one other time before. It had been with Alden when he traveled between the Otherworld and the world beyond.

Carissa gripped the mirror tighter. "She's an ankou."

"The ankou of the Deep Rhys." The washer woman whisked the two of them to the other side and then disappeared altogether.

Cameron shuddered. "Remind me to thank Alden for never being so terrifying."

Carissa could have reminded him about how terrified he'd been the first time they'd seen Alden in ankou form, but now wasn't the time for that. They walked back toward the marketplace, arms around each other. Carissa wanted to be angry at Cameron for coming here on his own, but she squeezed him tighter. Hiya and Cynth settled on him, getting orange all over his white shirt. That was punishment enough.

"Why did you come to see the washer woman? Didn't you know how dangerous it would be?" Carissa said.

"I overheard an elf talking to the bookseller. He was asking about a book."

"*Talisman of Tethra*?"

Cameron nodded. "That's the one. He asked about the talisman, said he was some kind of treasure hunter."

"I think I may have met him." Carissa recalled her encounter with the elves.

"And I think someone beat both him and us to the talisman. Cari, it has Tethra's magic in it. That's Tuatha de Danann magic. It's not just for protection, either. Do you see that fog?"

"You think someone created it with the talisman?" Carissa asked.

"It's a bit suspicious that it started right as Otto was killed, wouldn't you say? Look at the sky. Maybe the fog last night was natural, but that is not." He pointed to the thickening clouds.

He was right. The billowing gray sky looked anything but natural. Several shop keepers were packing up their carts early as the fog reached over the shoreline. Carissa and Cameron made it to the row where the road had begun, catching sight of the ship captain and several crewmates making their way toward the town.

"Captain!" Cameron held Carissa's hand tightly and quickened his step.

Logan turned back to meet them. "A storm is brewing. We'll take shelter here for the night."

Just behind Logan, Hela walked behind her floating luggage. She sped to a brisk walk in Carissa's direction. "Cari! Thank goodness you're all right. Did you see this terrible storm? Tabitha's hair is all frizzed, along with her puffy eyes. She's a terrible mess. Oh, here she comes."

Tabitha, rather than looking like the helpless widow Hela described her as, walked like a woman with a purpose. In all black, her green skin glowed. The spark in her fiery eyes spoke of anger more so than grief. Carissa was sure leaving her with Hela hadn't helped anything.

Hela waved her arm toward Carissa. "I've found her. See? She's all right."

Tabitha made no sign that she'd overheard Hela, but she locked eyes with Carissa and headed straight to her. She reached her hands out and pulled Carissa into a hug.

"Raven says Warren is still in custody," Tabitha whispered. "Otto's killer must've been someone on the ship."

Chapter 9

In Too Deep

Someone on the ship was a murderer. But who? On the one hand, Cameron swore he saw Warren the night Otto was killed, and on the other, the fog had already been so thick it was hard to know for sure that his senses hadn't tricked him. Furthermore, Raven had confirmed that the Ocean Reaper, Warren, was still in custody and had nearly arrived in Tir-Na-Nog. Warren couldn't be both Otto's killer and a prisoner in custody.

"So, who could you have seen at the time Otto was killed?" Carissa asked Cameron as they walked into the eerie fog with nothing but Carissa's elf-light.

Faerie dust swirled around the nature faeries as they floated between Carissa and Cameron. The last few stragglers in the marketplace stopped to watch their foolhardiness. Cameron and Carissa had no choice but to go back to the ship before they could rejoin the others at the inn. If Carissa hadn't sealed the room with her magic, the crew could have carried their luggage for them. Now they had to brave the fog alone.

"It was a silver cloak, like what the Ocean Reaper wears."

They neared the ship, walking through the magical barrier keeping out anyone other than the ship's crew and passengers. The air changed color around them, but the fog did not lift.

"Otto did pass away. Maybe MacLir assigned a new ocean reaper."

At the top of the gangway, the empty ship gave ghost vibes as the mist floated over the deck.

Cameron shuddered. "Could we not talk about this while we're alone on a ship with a skeleton crew?"

"You know that 'skeleton crew' doesn't literally mean there are skeletons on board," Carissa joked, but the faeries drew in closer to the couple. Their faerie dust lit the air as they shook.

Cameron held a palm open, holding Hiya like a lamp out in front of him. "I know, I'm just not sure why Logan would leave his ship with the water fae. Doesn't a captain always stay with his ship?"

"He trusts Beathan."

Carissa wasn't defending it, just trying to understand it herself. She knew too little of Beathan to draw any conclusions about her. It was just a feeling that she was hiding something.

A glimpse of movement toward the portside and then starboard told Carissa they were not alone. Cameron moved in closer, taking Carissa's hand. She squeezed it.

"No one but the *Scuabtuinne's* crew and passengers can get through the barrier."

"I know," he said. "Still, I'd rather not lose you in the fog."

They walked on like that until turning the corner. Nearing their cabins, Carissa caught sight of someone walking away from them. Though the visibility was low, Carissa made out a woman's form and the glint of a reflection coming off her dress. Then she remembered what Beathan had been wearing earlier that day.

The moment they opened the cabin door and stepped inside, Carissa asked, "Could it have been a woman you saw in silver?"

Cameron crossed the room and opened the closet. "I don't know, maybe. All I know is, it was a silver cloak. Why?"

"Beathan was wearing a silver dress and the way I saw her just now, I think she may have been the one you mistook for the Ocean Reaper."

"You think she was on deck when Otto was killed? Maybe she saw something."

"I don't think she's just a witness. You saw her near where Otto was killed. And instead of coming toward you, as the leader of the water fae crew should, she chose to leave in a hurry."

"Are you suggesting that she killed Otto?" Cameron's face spoke of disbelief and strain as he pulled out his suitcase.

Carissa's lips pulled to one side, "No, it's not enough information to draw that conclusion. But she does know something, at the very least. And we have to find out what."

Cameron took down a suitcase from Carissa's closet and opened it on her bed. Then he walked to his connecting room. Stopping short of his door, Cameron reached into his pocket and turned back.

"Oh, you'd better take the talisman. I have your grandfather's ring to protect me." The Claddagh engagement ring on his left finger was one Carissa had found recently in her grandfather's study. Once she'd noticed it was enchanted for protection, she immediately thought it could protect Cameron.

Carissa tugged at a necklace tucked under her shirt. She had worn the same circular, herb-filled pendant since she was a teenager. It not only allowed her to see into the Otherworld, but her mother had fortified it with her own Tuatha de Danann magic for added measure.

"This is a talisman, too. Really, you didn't need to ask for magical defenses for you and I on this journey," she said.

"Then we ought to give this to Sal, or perhaps Hela or Fen."

Cameron took the clamshell pendant out of his pocket and held it in his closed hand. Carissa could not keep her eyes off of it. A light engulfed his fingers.

"Cameron, look," she said.

The nature faeries flew over the talisman as Cameron opened his palm. Carissa moved forward. The light reflected in all their eyes like moonlight hitting water.

"Why is it glowing?" Cameron asked.

"It's detecting something," Carissa replied.

"Like what, an unseelie faerie?"

"Whatever it is, that's a danger signal."

Cameron gave her the talisman and hurried to throw some clothes in the suitcase.

"We'd better get to the inn before that danger finds us."

***

THE INN WAS filled with sailor's ballads and discussions of all the mysterious topics of the day. Druids and rhys dwfen alike engaged in guessing why the weather was turning and how long they might be staying at the inn. As for places to be stranded, the Deep Rhys Inn was not a bad find.

The lobby boasted a stone fireplace with a roaring fire, and a bar and restaurant with tables and chairs smoothly carved from what looked like boulders. Wooden beams overhead gleamed in the glow of firelight.

Sal sat in a corner, blowing his nose like a foghorn as the handkerchief waved between his fingers. Carissa sat beside him as Cameron took their belongings to their room. She laid a friendly hand between his shoulder blades.

"I heard you saw your parents' grave."

He nodded. "And I saw my cousins."

Carissa slid into the booth beside him. She waited as he hesitantly continued.

"They were packing up their shops. Raz, the bookkeeper, he said I shouldn't try to talk to them. And he was right."

"Why? What happened?"

Sal's eyes teared. "They packed up so fast, saying that they had nothing to give me. They didn't even let me explain that I didn't want anything from them."

"Why would they do that?" Carissa asked.

"Because they didn't want me near them, Cari."

"I'm sure that's not true." She squeezed his shoulder.

Shaking his head, he replied, "I could see it in their eyes how much they wanted me gone."

Carissa bit her lip, uncertain of what to say. It didn't fit with what she knew of rhys dwfen. The few she'd met had never so much as given a cross look. Now they were turning Sal away? Was that why Fudge had left, because his cousins were hard-hearted and mean? Were they scared of Sal? Or were they guilty of his parents' murder?

Three ice-cold mugs clunked together on the table in front of Carissa and Sal. Their sudden appearance caused Carissa to jolt back. She raised her eyes to the owner of the hand that had set them down. Raz bowed his head.

"Glad to see you and your friend survived your encounter with the washer woman, and perhaps you've come out the richer for it." Raz sat on the bench next to Sal.

"Have you met?" Sal glanced between them.

"Informally," Carissa nodded in something like a head bow. She hesitated but thought a polite response was warranted, given his help earlier. "I don't think I gave you my name. It's—"

"Carissa Shae," Raz finished. "Sal told me about his companions." Raz took a sip of his drink.

Sal sat up straighter and moved one mug toward Carissa while drawing the other toward himself. "Razzleberry was a friend of my parents," he explained.

Carissa had to get used to these rhys dwfen names. She'd always wondered why their names were all sweets. Sal told her once that all their real names were unpronounceable and ancient. The names they shared with the rest of the world were a means of showing others that they were sweet and kind-natured. Fudge had said because their true names were too infused with magic, they needed to be sealed behind frivolous ones. Carissa hadn't understood and Fudge had never explained any further. Now didn't seem like the time to discuss rhys dwfen name selection, however.

"How did you know Sal's parents?"

"He said it. We were friends," Raz said. Then a thoughtfulness fell over his eyes. He stared at the mug, reconsidering. "More like family, really. I grew up with Poppy and Fudge."

The way he tagged on Fudge's name at the end seemed curious. His voice had quieted to a whisper, almost like he hadn't wanted to mention his old friend. His eyes watered.

Sal clutched his mug. "I don't think it was murder. Otto was wrong. My cousins didn't want an investigation. And Raz tells me they donated the money to charities my mother loved and the jewels have never been touched. There's no motive then, is there? I've heard the sidhe talk about that—motive. If they wanted their money, why donate it? And if they wanted my mother's jewels, why not touch them for a hundred years?

"How do you know that they haven't?" Carissa asked.

"Raz was the executer of the will."

"And I'm happy to give you the jewels in my possession." said Raz.

"Thank you. And I think I'm glad to know there's nothing suspicious here. But I don't understand why my cousins don't want to see me." Sal took a sip and sighed.

Carissa didn't want to say that they might have had some other motive. Money wasn't the only reason to kill, as she'd learned over the last year. But Sal didn't need to hear that right now, and Carissa had no reason to believe his cousins were killers, other than their rudeness to Sal.

After taking a hefty gulp of his own drink, Raz set the mug down with a clack. "They loved your mother. Perhaps it's just painful to be reminded of her death."

"I wouldn't give up. Some of the merchants here did seem suspicious about what happened. And it is strange that your cousins are avoiding you." Carissa couldn't help but point that out, no matter how hard it might be for Sal to hear.

"No one was after your mother." Raz looked at Carissa with sharp eyes through his glasses.

"They might have been after his father then." Carissa challenged.

Raz took a deep breath in, then nodded. "Your father could not leave his old life as a pirate entirely behind. You'll likely hear a rumor somewhere about it if I don't tell you now. The whole town suspected that he still had some treasure—something other pirates would kill him to get. It's said he hid it somewhere on this island."

Carissa pushed her cup aside, leaning into the conversation. "Wouldn't it make more sense to kidnap him, then? They could interrogate him to find the treasure."

"Have you ever tried to interrogate a goblin? Lying is second nature to them—no offense to your father, rest his soul."

Sal's chin dipped. "If my father was a liar—"

Raz gripped Sal's wrist. "Oh no, he could be truthful when he wanted. I'm sure he was always honest with your mother. All I meant was that a goblin can hold onto a secret like no other when they want to keep truths hidden. For a pirate, it's easier to get rid of a goblin than to let them lead you down a winding trail of lies."

Carissa couldn't see how Raz's logic added up. "Crashing a boat into land seems excessive."

"Not if you want to take a whole family out in one fell swoop. Especially if this hidden treasure was locked away with blood magic. Then it would be impossible to get to without a blood relative to unlock it, or without the family gone entirely."

"My father locked a treasure away with blood magic?" Sal's eyes darted back and forth across the table as he took in this new information.

Carissa put an arm around his shoulder. She didn't want to cause him any further pain, but she had to ask, "What was this treasure?"

Raz shrugged. "No one knows. No one even knows if there was a treasure. This is all a theory. I don't believe it myself."

But the glint in his eyes told Carissa that Raz believed it entirely. He spoke with too much conviction for it to be gossip. And the way his eyebrows crinkled and his mouth sank down with a pitying look at Sal told Carissa he would not risk hurting Sal with idle rumors.

Carissa wouldn't let Sal suffer either, not when she could help it. Letting go of him, she leaned in close so only Raz and Sal could hear, "Cameron and I may have a way of finding out. A mirror into the past, so to speak."

"Something you acquired from the washer woman?" Raz asked.

Carissa nodded, then looked around. The lobby was filled with druids and rhys dwfen, all supposedly trustworthy. She would've said more, except that her eyes locked with the elf she'd seen this morning.

Sitting three tables away with his rough-housing companions, Neal raised his glass and lifted his chin in recognition. Carissa returned a strained smile. It wasn't suspicious for a traveling group of elves to stay at an inn, especially not the only one in town.

But all this talk of pirates connected in Carissa's mind. If ever she met a pirate in her life, she imagined he would be a lot like Neal. She looked away.

A more pleasant sight greeted her in the form of Cameron walking up to her table. She scooted closer to Sal, giving him a space to sit beside her in the curved booth. Cameron kissed her on the cheek and greeted the others.

"Hi, Sal. It's Raz, right?"

Raz nodded. The nature faeries settled atop Carissa's mug. She put a hand out to pull it away. Whatever frothy substance was in it, she was fairly certain it wasn't suitable for the sprites. Cameron, not fully paying attention, mistook the gesture as if she was handing it to him.

"Thanks." He took a sip and stared at the glass in awe. "What is this?"

"Golden Apple Foam." Raz sipped nonchalantly as Cameron delighted in another taste.

"If you like that, you ought to try the food. Fudge always said there are no better cooks in all the world." Sal raised a hand to catch a waiter's eye.

The sprites crossed their arms and glared at Carissa in unison. How was she to have known it wasn't something stronger? She still hesitated to order another when the waitress brought the menus. Carissa marveled at the choices as much as Cameron had at the drink.

Raz set his menu aside but watched Carissa and the nature faeries peering over theirs. "There's nothing here that would be harmful to the sprites. Everything that grows here is enchanted in the best sense. And every season is harvest time. It's one of the reasons our marketplaces are always busy."

"I've heard you have a plant that makes anyone invisible," Cameron referred to the flower Sal had mentioned the island was named after.

"We have more than that. But nothing in this restaurant will do that to you if that's what is worrying you." Raz's eyes twinkled with a hint of teasing.

"What makes you think I'm worried?" Cameron flipped his menu back to front and vice versa in his hands.

Nothing had made Carissa think he was nervous until he said that. She set her menu down. "What happened?"

"Nothing," he said.

She, Sal, and Raz stared in silence. Cameron glanced at each one of them. Then he slid his menu away.

"All right, but before I say anything, promise you won't be upset."

Carissa crossed her arms. There was no way in the Otherworld she was going to make such a promise. Chaos's frown told her it was bad news.

Cameron's shoulders drooped. "Logan agrees that it was probably a water fae who attacked Otto and put the warning in our suitcase, but not the ones who are part of the *Scuabtuinne's* entourage. He and Beathan's team are going to confront the water fae of the Deep Rhys tonight."

"I think that's a great idea," Carissa said.

"Wait, there's more. These water fae may be unseelie. Some might have a connection with Niall."

Carissa felt her heart beating faster, not from fear, but some mix of anger and determination. "That's fine. We can go with him to confront them."

Cameron put his hand atop her fingers. "Logan doesn't want you to go. Protecting you is his number one priority, and he thinks it would be safer if you stayed above the water."

"Safer?" Carissa lowered her voice, "It's safer for them if I go with them."

"You forget that every member of the crew is a druid. We will be fine."

"We?" Carissa felt the heat rising in her face.

Cameron's cheeks reddened. "I'm going with them."

"How is that safer?" Carissa asked.

Sal responded to her raising voice in his meek manner. "Captain Logan is a Tuatha de Danann. I'm sure he'll protect them."

The thought cooled the elfish sparks in her fingertips as she tapped the table. She could be much more rational about how much this journey meant to Cameron's self-discovery when she knew he wasn't putting himself in harm's way. She gave in.

"I suppose you're right."

Cameron put a hand on the back of his head. When he talked next, he spoke calmly. Still, Carissa knew that when he rubbed his neck like that, he was nervous about something.

"You'll see. I'll be an asset on that ship. I've been studying all the fae books I could since our troubles with the unseelie started. I've read all the books on water fae in your grandfather's study. I know my family history, including my water fae ancestors. And I was ambassador to Vale. I can help Logan negotiate."

Raz took his hat and stood. "You don't negotiate with water fae. Their natures are as changeable as the water, especially the unseelie."

"You're leaving?" Sal asked.

"It's one thing to talk of unseelie from decades ago and quite another to speak of meetings underwater with them now. I'm old, and my books are calling me. I live just up the corner. You can ask any of the locals where to find me if you should need me." He tipped his hat to them.

"He's right," Carissa said. "It's dangerous. Let me come with you."

"Come with you where? What's dangerous?" Hela's voice traveled over their heads. She and Fen came laden with shopping bags from the marketplace. They bumped into Raz on his way out. He stooped to pick up a bag Hela dropped.

Fen asked a waiter to bring over two more chairs. Carissa flashed a look at Cameron. The conversation about the unseelie was over. She wasn't about to put her pregnant friend through any further distress after Otto's death.

Hela sat back in the chair and thanked Raz for his help.

"I bought you gifts." She handed Cameron a bejeweled, sheathed knife, Sal a scarf, and Carissa a large tote she recognized from the spider-silk purse shop.

"You really didn't have to," Cameron said as he eyed the rusty blade.

"Thanks," Carissa said, examining her new seafoam green tote.

Sal said the same, though he seemed to genuinely appreciate his fall leaf scarf. He put it on right away. Somehow, it completed the restaurant's cozy atmosphere. Fen had not escaped the gifts either, judging by the nearly identical scarf around his neck.

"I'll take my leave." Raz chuckled as he said goodbye a second time.

"Oh, wait, are you one of Sal's cousins?" Hela asked.

"Just a friend."

Hela paid no mind to Raz's reply as she sifted through her gift bags. She pulled out a pumpkin orange ivy cap. The hue matched Sal's scarf but did not outdo the classic brown fedora already on Raz's head.

Hela pouted. "There weren't many shops open. Wait, I'm sure I have something else."

Raz replaced the hat, holding his old one on his head. "Not necessary, this is quite nice, thank you."

As Raz walked out of the restaurant, Carissa looked around. There was a person curiously absent among all water fae, elves, druids, and other visitors at the inn. Carissa had thought she'd been with Hela and Fen.

"Where is Tabitha?" she asked.

Hela looked over her menu. "She said she was going to take a nap. I wanted to invite her to come down for lunch, but she said not to bother her until dinner. I don't think she slept at all last night, the dear girl."

"I don't think any of us did," Carissa said.

Kind as Hela was and trusting as Fen was, neither of them thought anything was wrong in this situation. But the more Carissa thought about it, the more she realized that it wasn't likely Tabitha would be napping. She was high-strung and didn't much sleep on regular days, as she often said when she stayed for dinners far later than any other guests and beyond any length of time that would be considered normal. She may have said she would nap, but she'd told Carissa she planned to unpack.

Both might be true or neither. She might have simply not wanted company. Or perhaps Tabitha was up to something.

Chapter 10
Making Waves

Carissa finished her lunch as quickly as she could, and before the others had finished, she excused herself on the pretense of needing to rest. It would have been challenging to check on Tabitha otherwise, with the way Hela was treating Tabitha the way a mother hen would a chick. Perhaps Tabitha had told Hela she was sleeping just to keep herself from being smothered with "poor dears" and empty words about how everything was going to be all right.

Carissa would respect her decision if she needed some space, but she suspected Tabitha was not just taking time to grieve. She had been too worked up about Raven's response to just let it go. Tabitha suspected one of the crew and knowing her, she was setting out to find Otto's killer. Carissa should have realized it earlier.

She made it across the restaurant to the restrooms without Hela following her. In the hall to the stairs, however, she could no longer make her way up alone. Neal had apparently left his friends at their table to go to his room or to stalk her. She wasn't sure which.

"Carissa—did I remember that right?"

"Mmhmm." Carissa gave a tight-lipped smile.

"I couldn't help but overhear some of your conversation. My crew and I have dealt with water fae before. If your friends need a strong arm, well, I have some of the best men on the sea."

Carissa had used her own elf-ears to eavesdrop before, but she hadn't expected them to be listening. At least the elf seemed to want to help. She widened her smile politely.

"Thank you, but I'm sure they'll be fine." Carissa resumed walking.

Neal swerved to get in front of her. His smile remained friendly as he leaned an arm to the wall to block her path. "You did not seem so confident a minute ago. Your friend is human, am I right? Descendent of a water fae, I understand, but you and I both know a human is nothing against a fae. Unless he's a druid?"

Carissa crossed her arms. "He has fought against unseelie before and won. And he's not my friend, he's my fiancé." She flashed her Claddagh engagement ring for emphasis.

Neal's eyes widened, and he let go of the wall. His arms fell to his sides. It was a universal look of disappointment, and for a moment Carissa regretted how harshly she'd said it.

"Sorry, I didn't realize...I..." He bowed his head. "The offer still stands. Whenever you ask, I'm at your service."

"Thank you," she replied, almost as if it were an apology.

They walked their separate ways. Carissa's face flushed more and more as it sunk in that she'd misunderstood Neal. She'd seen him as suspicious, just as she'd seen everyone else. Beathan, Logan, she'd even assumed that some of the more eccentric-looking druids were secretly unseelie. She may have been right about Neal having ulterior motives, but based on his reaction to her relationship status, she'd been wrong about the motive itself. That eased her mind a little as she reached the second floor and passed one of Neal's elves in the hallway. He was much friendlier now—too friendly. He smirked in recognition, and she felt his eyes trailing her as she walked by. Carissa rolled her eyes. At least he hadn't catcalled.

A few rooms down, she found Tabitha's suite. She knocked gently.

No answer.

She tried again. "Tabitha?"

Again, there was no response. Carissa looked left and right. In the empty hallway, it was safe to use her elf-light to unlock the door. A magical barrier stopped her.

Either the hotel had formidable charms protecting the doors or Tabitha had sealed the room herself. Perhaps she'd even soundproofed it.

Rather than knock again, Carissa decided to take a look at her own room since it was right next door. Her key slipped into the lock smoothly, but the door came away without her turning the lock or the knob. Carissa was sure that wasn't how any locks worked, even enchanted ones.

The door was open, and the lock broken. Carissa pushed the door all the way. She took one step inside and saw that the room was torn apart. The pillows and blankets had been ripped from the bed. The cabinets turned inside out, and the nightstand was empty.

Carissa hastened to it, bending down to see what she could recover. The book was there. She went around the room, surveying all the clothes and accessories scattered in disarray. Only one item appeared to be missing: the mirror. Carissa abandoned the place and pounded more frantically on Tabitha's door.

"Tabitha it's Cari. If you're in there, please open the door."

She tried her Tuatha de Danann magic this time. A stream of mauve-tinted smog enveloped the lock. The knob turned. Carissa pounded through the door shoulder first, knocking it open.

The room appeared untouched. The covers lay flat on the bed, the dresser shone with dust-free radiance, and the light streaming in from the windows settled on two unopened suitcases lined up perfectly beside the restroom door. That was the only sign of an occupant.

Tabitha was gone.

***

"IT TOOK MORE than my elf-light to open that door."

Not wanting to disturb the whole hotel, Carissa led only Cameron and Logan to the room. But because it was unavoidable to keep Hela away from the action, she and her husband came along.

"Well, of course. The innkeeper told us when we checked in that the seals were unbreakable."

Hela did not know how to keep a low tone. Thankfully, the halls were still bare for the moment. Logan moved to the front.

"Rhys dwfen magic is powerful, but it can be broken without Tuatha de Danann magic," he said.

Carissa glanced at Cameron. "What kind of magic could do it?"

"Any magic if skilled enough, even elf-light." Logan held his hand out to Room 205 and stepped aside, eyes resting on Fen.

Hela pulled a key out of her purse. "We don't need magic to open our own door."

Fen tapped her wrist gently. "I think he'd like us to demonstrate his point."

Hela mouthed an "oh" and slid her key back in the silk purse. Not soon after the bag closed, Fen, with both hands out in front of him, lit up the lock with bright white elf-light. A click sounded, and Hela pushed her way through the door.

"Impossible," Carissa said.

"Forgive me, but Cameron told me about your upbringing. You weren't properly trained in elf-light magic, is that right?" Logan asked.

Cameron avoided looking at her as she glanced in his direction.

"That's true," she had to admit.

"There was a suspicious group of elves downstairs. Pirates by the look of them," Logan said.

"Sailors," Carissa corrected. "I met them earlier today."

"And did they know you were with the *Scuabtuinne?*" Logan asked.

Carissa thought back. She hadn't explicitly said it, but she couldn't be certain that they hadn't seen the *Scuabtuinne* arriving.

"I'm not sure," she said. "I did see one in the hallway earlier."

"Then perhaps that is who broke into your room," Logan concluded.

Hela and Fen clicked the door shut as they exited.

"Nothing is the matter in our room," Hela informed.

"Let's see the damage in ours," Cameron said.

Logan took the lead. Since the lock was already broken, the door swung aside with a tap of his hand. Logan took a few steps forward. The rest of them followed.

Carissa squeezed past all of them. Making her way around the bed, she pointed to the nightstand. Cameron shared a nod with her. She would not reveal to the others about the missing mirror, but at least Cam had understood.

"What did you have of value?" Logan asked.

"Nothing here." Carissa spied the book on Rhys Dwfen treasures on the floor.

Hela gasped, thankfully not at the book. She was still taking in the room as a whole. "My goodness, was Tabitha's room like this, too?"

"No, but she wasn't in her room. She's missing."

Carissa picked up the book and held it nonchalantly. She leaned on the wall near the window and placed it down on the windowpane so the spine wouldn't show. Logan might think it suspicious to find one of the books from his library in her possession.

Hela stepped around a pile of clothes and sank on to the bed, rubbing her belly. "Missing? That's a bit dramatic. I'm sure she just went for a walk or some fresh air."

Dramatic? For all these years, Carissa had always thought Hela lacked the self-awareness to see how perfectly that word fit her. Carissa had never known Hela to be anything but dramatic.

Cameron opened the curtain wide enough for the room's attention to drift out the window.

"Fresh air in that?" he asked.

The question was valid. No one would go for a walk in the current condition. Even Tabitha had enough sense to stay indoors given what they could, or rather couldn't, see. Magic was everywhere tonight.

The fog had enveloped the town.

Chapter 11

Ocean Alliances

"We will have a team of our own water fae with us. Everything will be fine," Cameron assured.

"Who do you mean? Gerard? He's here to pay for a crime he already committed." Carissa folded up clothes in sync with Cameron, replacing them in the dresser.

"You agreed with me at the time that Gerard was manipulated into helping an unseelie. He even warned us about the water fae."

Carissa handed him the last shirt and let out a frustrated grumble. "That's what I'm worried about. We don't know anything about Beathan or her team. If they betray you—"

Cameron slid the dresser drawer shut. Turning to Carissa, he put both hands on her shoulders and pulled her close. She hugged him tight.

"Stop worrying. For the last time, we will be fine." Cameron kissed her forehead.

Carissa let go. She did not push the argument about going with him. Instead, she had plans to stick close by. She said, "All right, I will look around the island for Tabitha."

"Do *I* need to worry about *you*?" Cameron kept his arms locked around her a moment longer.

Carissa smiled. "I'll have the sprites with me, and I'm fairly sure that no matter how much I tell them to stay, Sal and Hela will be with me."

"Hela should really stay at the hotel."

"If one of us tells her one more time that 'it's not good for the baby,' I'm afraid she'll go right into attack mode."

He laughed. "I suppose Hela is not one to be told to sit out of the action."

"Hela doesn't have anything to do but worry or tag along. But I fear that it will be dangerous for her. I'd much rather provide her with some sort of distraction."

"Or she may be stronger than you think. It might not be a terrible idea for her to be with you instead of you going out there alone."

"You're only saying that because you're concerned for me," Carissa said.

"Always." Cameron and Carissa shared one final kiss before he left to meet the crew downstairs.

Alone in the room, Carissa readied the sprites for the long night ahead. "You know I'd rather have the two of you stay safe in the room, but since you are going to wander around anyway, listen closely. I want Hela, Fen, and Sal distracted. Keep them here if you can, or if they insist on going exploring, maybe you can get Hela to take Sal and try contacting his cousins again. Or maybe Sal can find out where Raz's home is, and they can reminisce some more about his parents. Anything is fine, but keep them safe and don't let them follow me. I'm trusting you two to do that."

Hiya saluted, but Cynth pointed at Chaos. Carissa frowned. She glanced at Chaos sternly so the little sprite wouldn't brag.

"I'm sorry, but I may need Chaos with me."

To her credit, Chaos gave Hiya and Cynth a sympathetic look. A few months back she might have been doing somersaults for getting special treatment, but since they'd become closer friends, Chaos was learning to treat Hiya and Cynth more gently. With a long face, Cynth nodded and pulled Hiya toward the door, which Carissa opened just a crack for them to leave.

Then she grabbed a black hooded shirt, borrowed from Cameron's informal apparel, and pulled it over her head. She lifted the hood and tapped the left side of the cloth.

"Come on, Chaos. I've got an idea where Tabitha is, and she might be in trouble. If anyone sees us, I'd like your being with me to be a surprise."

Chaos nodded and entered the space Carissa had made for her in the corner of the hood. Once Chaos had climbed inside, Carissa pulled the hood's strings tight and tied it. Chaos sat snugly against Carissa's chin, peering out from the edge of the fabric.

"Let's go find our friend in distress."

***

THE *SCUABTUINNE* TOOK on an eerie form in the fog, like a Fata Morgana in the sky. Only after she'd approached the dock did she see that the boat rested serenely on the water. The gangway rocked gently with the ship.

She made it through the boat's protective barrier easily. Once again, the deck was deserted. This time, without Cameron there, every creaking sound on the ship sent a shiver right down Carissa's spine. Chaos scrunched the hood around her. Carissa gagged and tapped the nature faerie lightly until she let go of her death grip.

"Easy," Carissa whispered, as much to herself as to the sprite.

Across the deck and near the stairs leading to Tabitha's room, Carissa could hear not only creaks but wind, water, and distant whispers in the dark. She steeled herself with a deep breath and stepped down, one foot at a time, with little enough weight on each forward motion as she could manage. The metal stairs made no sound discernable from the rest of the ship the entire way until her feet landed on Tabitha's floor.

The halls were empty, though Carissa wondered if she would hide if there were a person ahead. She had every right to be here, as did any member of the crew. Carissa should have had nothing to fear. Except that one of them might be a murderer.

Tabitha's room was locked. Rather than knocking this time, she attempted to use her Tuatha de Danann magic to break the changeling spell Tabitha had placed on it. Only she didn't get that far.

A hooded figure appeared at her left, hands glowing in a purple mist of magic. Carissa turned, and Chaos escaped the hoodie, charging her own hands with faerie dust. The Tuatha de Danann magic had already ignited at Carissa's palms, but she hesitated to use it.

Purple shot toward her, and she held her palm up to deflect, all the while thinking the magic was familiar. Recognition hit her as the hooded figure's second attack wrapped the magic around Carissa's waist. Chaos's faerie dust shot the hooded figure in the face, and the holding broke. The coughing figure could have been caught off guard, but Carissa walked forward instead.

"Tabitha?" she whispered.

The figure coughed a few more times and lowered her hood. Green eyes blinked back at her.

"Cari? What are you doing here?"

The nature faerie pointed at Tabitha and crossed her arms, demanding the same question of her. Tabitha stepped forward.

"Sorry, but how was I to know it was you?"

Carissa didn't argue that there was no fog below deck and she could perfectly well see her red hair since she wasn't wearing a hood. Instead, she relaxed her stance and encouraged Chaos with a look to do the same. On her shoulder, Carissa could feel Chaos's left foot tapping as she waited for a full explanation from Tabitha. Carissa helped her along.

"We were worried when we didn't see you in your room at the inn. Why did you come here alone?"

Tabitha grabbed her hand and led her down the hall. In a room that was not her own, Tabitha ushered Carissa and Chaos to have a seat. It didn't feel right making herself comfortable in some crewmate's room, so Carissa stood and repeated her question.

Tabitha answered as if the walls had elf-quality ears. "Raven sent me on this mission."

In a regular voice, Carissa responded, "I know. She told me herself."

"No, you don't understand. Raven sent me on this mission."

Tabitha waved her arms in circles, but the meaning was lost on Carissa. Chaos scratched her head, too.

"This mission? Snooping around the ship?" Carissa asked.

Tabitha tapped Carissa's nose. "Exactly."

Putting a hand to her forehead, Carissa said, "Tabitha, I'm sorry. I'm not following. What is your mission, exactly?"

With a frustrated "ugh" preceding it, Tabitha gave her explanation, "To search the crew's quarters. Raven thought there was a spy aboard."

Technically, going through the crewmate's things meant Tabitha was the spy, but Carissa knew what she meant. She couldn't help but wonder if Tabitha had misunderstood, however. It was hard to believe that something that important hadn't been told to her directly from Raven herself.

"When did Raven tell you this?" Carissa had to assume it had been in her recent letter.

"Before we ever came on this mission. She worried specifically about the water fae. Raven thinks one of them works for Niall Shae."

"She never said anything to me."

"If she had, what would you have done?"

Carissa opened her mouth to argue, but she saw her point. The first thing Carissa would have done is exactly what Tabitha had and moved to a room below. Then she'd have snuck into the rooms—specifically Beathan's. But since most of the crews' attention would be on Carissa, it would have been harder for her to do her spying. She might not have gotten away with it. Maybe Otto hadn't gotten away with it either.

"Was Otto helping you? Do you think the spy killed him for discovering him?" Carissa asked.

"No, well, I mean, maybe, but Otto wasn't helping me. I really meant it when I told him not to come. I don't know why he wouldn't listen to me." Tabitha's chin trembled, straining not to cry.

Carissa bit her lip. Even though she knew the reason, she was not sure that now was the right time to tell Tabitha. Rather than make her feel better, it might only shift her emotions toward blaming Sal. It wouldn't be rational, but grief, like any strong emotion, was not a matter of rationality.

Tabitha controlled her mood well enough when focused on the mystery, so Carissa redirected her attention there.

"So there's a water fae traitor on board. Who do you suspect?"

"No one yet." Tabitha threw her hands up. "It's so hard. I tried detecting magic, but there's magic everywhere." Carissa hadn't thought about detecting magic. She couldn't do so herself anyway. Changlings could sense others in ways no other fae could. Their bonds with others, their emotions, and their magic. Even Chaos looked at Tabitha with fascination as she continued, "I wanted to see if there was a crewmate's room that had some unexpected magic or more magic than they should, but I studied all the rooms and the ones with the strongest magic are exactly the ones you would expect."

"Which ones are those?"

Tabitha counted on her fingers, "Beathan's, then Logan's, then the head water fae's, then the chief druid's—"

"Wait, go back. Why did you say Beathan's name first?"

Tabitha shrugged. "Her room has the most powerful magic."

"Isn't that unusual?"

"Why?"

"Logan is the captain. He has the Immortal Flame in his room that powers the whole ship. Why wouldn't his cabin have the most magic?"

"Oh! Oh, I see! Doesn't he have an engine room like Jane's ships? Never mind, if Beathan's room has more powerful magic than the Immortal Flame, she might've smuggled something on board."

Carissa nodded. Logan had worried that the immortal flame might not be powerful enough to protect the ship. But if Beathan had so much power, Logan wouldn't have to worry. Why would she hide that from him? Carissa had to find out.

"I think we should have a look at Beathan's cabin."

"That'll be easy. We're in Beathan's room now."

"Excellent." Carissa began looking around.

Chaos beat her to it. She struggled with her faerie dust to open Beathan's nightstand drawer. Carissa walked over, using her Tuatha de Danann magic to form a pink cloud over the lock. The cloud twisted to a whirlwind, which inserted itself in the lock and turned.

"Okay, but, Cari?" Tabitha interrupted again.

"Wait just a moment," Carissa said. Inside the dresser lay a jewelry box. Inside it was a necklace made of glittery blue stone in the shape of a dolphin's tail. Carissa lifted it carefully. The way the gleam shifted from one end to the other as if under a spotlight made it clear this had to be an object of magic. A talisman, perhaps?

"Cari, is now a good time to tell you that someone is coming this way?"

Chapter 12

Red Herring

Carissa should have heard the footsteps. She peeked outside the doorway. *A druid or a water fae?* She struggled to see until the person stepped under the nearest light in the hallway. A druid with shoulder-length reddish-brown hair and a beard approached them. Carissa handed the talisman to Tabitha and sealed the door.

"He may not know we're here. We'll just wait for him to pass and then leave."

A fist pounded on the door. "You may as well come out, I've already seen you, Miss Shae, Miss Tabitha. There are traces of changeling magic on every lock in this hallway."

Carissa shot a worrisome half-smile Tabitha's way. Tabitha shrugged and mouthed, "Sorry." With no other choice, Carissa undid the seal with a handwave, but before she opened the door, Tabitha held her hand back.

"Identify yourself."

"My name is Ennis. I am the druid assigned to night shift for this section."

Carissa rested a palm on Tabitha's hand and looked at her as she gently moved it away. She tried to convey with her eyes that it was okay. She also gave Chaos her stern face, which Chaos knew meant she should stay out of sight. She hid herself in Tabitha's hair, in case they needed a surprise attacker.

Carissa opened the door and Ennis bowed his head, a hand resting on the hilt of his sword. His eyes narrowed as he smiled. Carissa tensed at the subtle interplay between respectfulness and hostility.

"I've seen you before, you warned me about the kelpie."

"Yes, I believe I did. Ladies, please forgive me, but I must ask what you are doing in Mistress Beathan's quarters."

"We are looking for the traitor who killed my husband!"

Carissa put a hand out to calm Tabitha and to keep Ennis from taking her yelling as an attack. Mostly, her hand wave was meant to hide Chaos from view. The ready-for-fisticuffs faerie took the hint and traveled behind Carissa, who could feel a pinch on her neck telling her Chaos was holding on to the hood. Tabitha crossed her arms. The druid's hand let go of the sword hilt.

With a sense of calmness restored, Carissa said, "We meant no harm, but we are here on a mission to discover proof of a possible traitor."

Ennis's mouth dropped. "You found evidence of treachery in Mistress Beathan's quarters? I cannot believe it."

"Ye—" Tabitha began.

"No," Carissa said firmly. "We didn't find anything. But we would like to keep looking if that's all right."

Ennis thought for a moment. "I'm sorry. If a search is not authorized by the captain, I don't think I can allow you to continue. I can accompany you on a search of all the main areas."

He held a hand out, gesturing for them to leave Beathan's room. Carissa silenced Tabitha's protests with a look and Chaos's pinching with a hand to her neck, swatting her lightly on the bum. Chaos stopped, though Carissa imagined she'd throw a temper tantrum later.

Carissa, and eventually Tabitha, followed Ennis down the hallway. They traveled to the lower deck's common room. Tabitha and Ennis used their magic to scan what looked like a billiards board, some type of shuffleboard, a target for shooting arrows, and a bar. The surprisingly modern design contrasted with a tree growing in the back the room, its roots traveling upward to create what Carissa assumed was a climbing wall.

Carissa physically opened and shut the cupboards and cabinets of the bar, following Ennis's magical examination. It was powerful magic. Carissa felt it reverberating through the air with such intensity she swore she could see light particles vibrating around her. Even elf eyes were not supposed to detect magic like that.

She was learning to expect that from druids. Humans surprised her every day with the power of their magic. They seemed to have none but had more than even they could imagine. Druids like Jane and Ennis were prime examples.

Her thoughts on druid magic distracted her until she felt Chaos's little hands smacking her cheek. She looked down.

The talisman around her neck was glowing. She quickly tucked it under her shirt. The glow stopped or was no longer visible. Carissa peered into the hallway. Whatever danger the talisman was sensing, she couldn't see a cause.

Ennis's voice called out, "I'm finding nothing out of the ordinary. Perhaps if you'll tell me what we're looking to find?"

"Anything suspicious," Tabitha said.

Carissa had a better idea of what to ask. "Ennis, have you heard of a Talisman of Tethra?"

A flicker of recognition passed over his eyes.

"Yes, supposedly a talisman holding power to protect one from any magic on the seas."

"Does it have any negative repercussions?"

"Negative repercussions? You mean, can it attack anyone? No, it's strictly protective."

Ennis was dismissive, but Carissa could recall the washer woman's words as if she were standing at the river. She'd warned that one talisman, the one she was wearing now, would protect her, and the other, the Talisman of Tethra, would lead to someone's death. She had to know what the washer woman had meant.

"That's not what I mean. Is it cursed or charmed in some way?"

"I'm not aware of any curse. Who told you that?" Ennis asked.

Carissa responded hastily. "No one, never mind that. Do you know what the talisman looks like?"

"It would be a necklace with some kind of symbol of the sea."

"Like a dolphin's tail?"

"Possibly. It's so ancient no one actually knows what it looks like, just that it would be so powerful, one would be able to feel the magic coming off of it. It would have to be kept in a mistletoe-lined box to avoid being detected. But I doubt it would be on board. The last anyone knew of the talisman, it had been taken from Tethra's wife by a jealous water fae. It has been lost since."

Carissa watched Tabitha rattling through every one of the drawers. Chaos was shooting each lock with faerie dust to help. Now Carissa was certain they would not find the pendant there.

"Which Tuatha de Danann woman owns it?"

"I'm sorry. Druids are not privy to that information. There are some legends the Tuatha de Danann keep only among themselves."

Tabitha slammed a drawer. "Nothing."

Chaos tangled herself back into Tabitha's hair, and Tabitha bounded over as if ready to pounce on the next room. Carissa winced at the exuberance and at how conspicuous Chaos's round eyes were as she blinked between gold strands.

Subtly nodding, Carissa said, "Thank you for your help, Ennis. I think we may have been on the wrong track. We'll leave the ship to you and the other druids."

As Ennis bowed and showed them out of the room, Tabitha walked close to Carissa, whispering, "We're going to keep looking on our own, aren't we?"

Carissa waited until they'd rounded a corner, losing Ennis as he diverged the other way. "We don't have to keep looking. I think we found it in Beathan's room. Remember that necklace?"

"This one?"

Tabitha pulled the silver chain with the blue dolphin's tail pendant out of a hidden pocket in her dress. Carissa hadn't expected Tabitha to swipe the item when she'd handed it to her earlier. At least they wouldn't have to go back for it. Carissa clasped Tabitha's hands and pushed the pendant down.

"Keep it hidden."

"But what is it? Is this what was used to kill Otto?"

Tabitha placed the talisman back in her pocket.

Carissa made a whooshing motion with her arms to urge Tabitha forward.

"I'll tell you everything once we're at the hotel."

***

SAFELY SEATED AT a secluded table tucked into a corner by a window, Carissa watched rain clouds threaten the island while Tabitha processed Carissa's revelation. Chaos sat with her hand on her chin and her nose scrunched up, considering Carissa's theory. After a long while watching a few drizzles on the glass, Tabitha spoke.

"I don't understand. If the talisman is supposed to kill you—"

"Shh! Tabitha, I never said it would kill *me*. The washer woman said it would kill someone close to him, someone 'as good as family.'"

Tabitha's eyebrows chastised her as if saying *"that's obviously you,"* but she continued in a softer voice, "All right, so it will kill someone. But aren't talismans meant to protect?"

"I don't know how it leads to a person's death. Maybe a spell will bounce off of it and hit the spellcaster. Maybe the magic in it is cursed to anyone but the proper wearer. Who knows? There has to be a reason Beathan isn't wearing it herself."

"And you think that Beathan stole it from a powerful woman?"

"A Fomorian. They were once almost as formidable as the Tuatha de Danann. We haven't heard about them in centuries, but that doesn't mean they're all gone. For all I know, the original owner might seek vengeance, and someone might die when she tries to reclaim the talisman."

"I don't understand what this has to do with Otto's death."

Carissa looked out the window, thinking. Otto could have found out about the talisman from one of the books in the library. She wasn't sure how he could have linked that to Sal's parents' death—unless the talisman was somehow listed among Grem's and Poppy's possessions. Perhaps it was the treasure Grem had hidden on the island and Beathan had found it here. The only thing she knew for a fact was that someone or something had been on board the *Scuabtuinne* today that had caused the washer woman's talisman to glow. Without having any definitive proof, and knowing how rashly Tabitha sometimes acted, Carissa preferred not to say more for now.

"Maybe it's nothing. I'm sorry, Tabitha. I don't think we're any closer to discovering Otto's killer." Carissa put a hand on Tabitha's arm.

They both looked up when bells above the inn door rang. Carissa hoped it was Cameron, but it was too soon to be him. Instead of the captain and crew returning, in walked Sal, Hela, and Fen, shaking raindrops off of their heads. Sal held the door for the others, then wrung his scarlet scarf before entering. Hela opened her purse for two dry sprites to fly out, unaffected by the weather.

The three of them spotted Carissa and Tabitha immediately but took their time walking over. All of them wore long faces. Hela's handkerchief worked double time between the rain and her tears.

Carissa straightened, asking, "What's wrong?"

"Excuse me. It's been a long day, and I'm tired." Sal bowed and bounded away in long strides.

Carissa's and Tabitha's eyes moved from him to Hela. Fen, knowing his wife well enough by now, walked to the bar to order some dinner as his wife expressed her embellished version of events. Hela pushed her way into the booth beside Tabitha.

"Tabitha, thank goodness she found you!"

"Was I lost?" Tabitha tilted her head, befuddled as Hela and Fen sat down.

Hela ignored her, "It was horrible! Oh, no more horrible than what you went through, you wretched thing."

Hela forced an arm around Tabitha's shoulders. Then she let go to blow her nose into her already soaked handkerchief. Cynth and Hiya covered their ears and flew to the other side of the booth to share Chaos's dinner. Carissa gave Tabitha a sympathetic smile as she waited for Hela to continue.

"We were looking for you, of course. But then I told Sal we ought to go see his cousins." Carissa shot a glance at Hiya and Cynth. The faeries were rolling their eyes. They'd led Hela to the idea. Hela rubbed her baby bump as she continued, "You would think family would be there for you. No matter what the cruel worlds do, family is supposed to help you. Even if they've never met you, especially then, they should welcome you with open arms. 'No one is more welcoming than the rhys dwfen.' Well, I'll never place my trust in a stereotype again. Who knew they could be so unreliable?"

Carissa caught the death stare on Tabitha's face. She met it with a headshake to try to convince her not to act on it. Stereotypes were the whole reason she'd nearly been condemned just for being a changeling a few months ago. Hela, as always, was oblivious to the thoughtlessness of her words.

Picking up on the point of Hela's rant, Carissa asked, "Sal's cousins turned him away again?"

"They practically threw him out of their houses, which conveniently are all on the same street. At least that made it easier to take the rejections. Each of them said that they did not want any trouble and to leave them be. They would not give him his inheritance and told him that if he had any questions, he would have to ask the 'foreboding bookseller who kept his parents' secrets.'"

"Who?" Tabitha asked.

"Someone named Raspberry or something like that. The one who was leaving as we arrived at the inn."

"Raz," Carissa said.

Raz was the executer of their will. But why would the cousins call him foreboding? And what secrets did they mean? It did not take long for Hela to give her theory.

"This Raz person obviously wants the treasure for himself. One of the cousins told us he pretended to be some kind of adventurer, selling rare books and artifacts from his many 'adventures,' but he never left the island. His parents were travelers. Now he just trades with visitors without ever leaving the island. He's a phony and probably already has Sal's treasures in his possession. From what I hear, he's rich enough but miserly about spending any of it. He's a greedy fraud if you ask me."

Carissa wasn't sure he was motivated by greed considering how he'd warned against the treasure or how eagerly he said he'd return Sal's mother's jewels. Hela hadn't even met him before formulating an opinion, but the idea that the treasure lay in his possession might not be far off. He had a collection of rare artifacts, whether he'd inherited, traded, or discovered them himself. And he had been friends with Grem and Poppy, so it might be possible that he had their treasure this whole time – *or killed them for it?* Carissa decided she'd finish her dinner, but afterward, she'd pay a visit to Raz and find out precisely what he was hiding.

Chapter 13

High Tides and Alibis

Raz's home was brick for brick as the waitress in the inn had described it. "A quaint mini-castle built for one," she'd said. That it was.

All the way down on the corner one road away from the inn, a sign on an antique mailbox read *Bookseller & Antique Trader*. It was fading as if written a century ago, yet the home appeared to be well-kept.

The stonework rose into a rectangular tower from which light emanated through a curved window at the top. The tower formed the entryway to a mini house with a curtained window, and beside it rested a bicycle attached to a covered caravan cart. This was no doubt the same cart that had expanded to become Raz's shop in the marketplace.

Carissa used the knocker, a scaled-down brass nautical anchor, and knocked three times. She felt a shadow creep into the corner of her eye, but it darted away as she tried to view it. The lack of light at the end of this street gave the whole home an eerie feel.

The door inched open, and Raz's bespectacled eyes appeared in the thin space. The door shut. Carissa pushed a hand on the solid wood, but the slinking sound of the chain told her Raz was only opening the door. With a final clink, the door reopened.

"Miss Shae, you came here alone?"

Carissa pulled her hood tighter around her head. It was more comfortable without a sprite smothered in the neckline. She'd settled the sprites to bed before going out. There was no need to keep them up, and the rain was not good for their collective health. The rain was light enough now to be classified as a drizzle. It was still enough to make the September air feel cold.

"You said we should feel free to visit if we have any questions," she said.

"Yes, of course, come in out of the fog."

Raz moved with the door, letting her push past. He lingered a moment before closing it, peering outside and looking up at the sky. Once the door snapped into place, he took out a handkerchief and patted his forehead.

"May I fix you a cup of tea?"

"No, thank you." Carissa did not waste time on formalities. "Raz, why did you tell Sal's cousins to send him away?"

Raz's eyes traveled away from Carissa. She followed his gaze the short distance between his sofa chair and his stove. Though the living room, kitchen, and study shared a single open space, the materials appeared to be high-end—from oak hardwood floors to marble counters. The human-made designs would be considered rare in a fae community. Carissa wondered if he'd afforded the luxuries from his work or Sal's inheritance.

Raz said, "I think I'll have a tea myself."

But he didn't move to the stove. Instead, he let himself rest on the bench beside the front window. He looked tired, as if he lacked the strength to put on a kettle. Carissa, still unsure how much of this was an act, stood in front of him.

"You did tell Sal's cousins not to speak with him, didn't you?" She crossed her arms for greater effect.

Raz ran a trembling hand through his hair. He closed his eyes and spoke in a soft voice, "I'm just trying to protect everyone."

"From what?" Carissa asked.

Raz looked up. "Everything I told you was true. The treasure is cursed. There is nothing here for you. Leave it be, I beg you. Leave the island."

"So that you can have the treasure for yourself? Sell off any items of value and buy a fine house like this?"

He shook his head as if in pain. "No. I would never."

"Raz, you are an excellent bargainer and have traded many rare artifacts with travelers, but I know you've never left this island. And I don't think you wanted us to come here."

Now his eyes met hers sharply. He looked away just as quickly.

Carissa put her hands on her hips, continuing, "Sal sent his cousins a letter well before we left Moss Hill. You knew we were coming. You told Sal's cousins not to speak to him, and when you met Sal, you told him not to talk to them. You wanted to keep them apart."

Hanging his head low, he said, "Why didn't you just sail away from the fog?"

Like the blasting horn of an incoming ship, the realization struck her then.

"You created the fog, didn't you? You have the talisman. Sal's parents left it with you—no, wait. There's more to it. You know about rare artifacts. You knew about the washer woman and the talisman." Carissa started pacing as Raz stared at the floor, not denying a word. "The washer woman said that someone else had asked for the talisman, someone who knew about it. It was you. Wasn't it? Did the washer woman have the talisman to give you, or did she tell you how to get it? Did you enlist Sal's father to find the treasure for you?"

Raz took a deep breath. "Sal's father, Grem, had visited the island more than once before striking up a romance with Fudge's sister. He sometimes brought treasures to trade in my shop. He found the talisman with my help. I asked the washer woman for a map that led to its discovery. I gave the map to

Grem. We were overjoyed when he did, but when we realized how powerful it was, we knew we could not use it nor sell it."

"You didn't keep it quiet, though, did you? By then, people were talking about it."

Raz sobbed. Between deep breaths, he managed, "No, no, I said nothing. Still, some pirates found out about it somehow, perhaps on Grem's journeys. When I found out he was killed for it…"

Carissa pressed, but in a gentler voice, saying, "He was killed because it was sealed with blood magic?"

Raz reddened. "I misled you. The only possession Sal's parents had that worked by inherited—what do you humans call them, genes?—is a good luck charm Sal already has with him. He's had it since he was a babe. It might be the only reason he wasn't also killed by the pirates."

"Forgive me, but how do I know they weren't killed by *you?*"

Carissa believed the shock that showed in the lines around his eyes and his open-mouth stare. He seemed genuinely hurt by her question. She felt the guilt swell in her heart for causing him such pain—if he was innocent. If he was guilty, his own words would convict him.

"I was with Fudge that day. He can tell you if you don't believe me.I'm not a fae who would harm a fly. Most especially not any member of that family."

Raz walked back to the window. There was something, a melancholy longing in his voice. The way he sunk into the chair made it seem like he was still mourning. Carissa wouldn't have pried but was still trying to gauge whether she could trust him.

"You were more than friends with Poppy, weren't you?"

"No, not remotely." Raz gave a strangled laugh that turned into a sob. "I couldn't return that kind of affection with her."

"That's why your relationship with her ended, and she married Grem?"

Raz shook his head. "You don't understand. I was never with her. I never wanted to be with *her*."

There was something in the way Raz said it, something that clicked with things he'd said before. Carissa searched her memory, finding a phrase, a word, a tone he'd used. It was the tone he'd used whenever he'd said Fudge's name.

Carissa moved closer, speaking softly, "You were in love with Fudge."

His eyes welled. It was all the confirmation Carissa needed. She sat beside him on the bench.

"Since we were fifty years old. I knew I loved him even then." Raz used his handkerchief to dry his eyes.

"Sal told me once that Fudge hadn't fit in," Carissa said.

Raz looked at her curiously. Even through tears, he smiled. "You assume that's because he was in love with me?"

"Isn't it?"

"I've heard that humans think like that. No. By that logic, I wouldn't be accepted here, and I very much am."

"So, then what set him apart?"

"Rhys dwfen only judge each other by one criterion: How kind we are to others and to ourselves. Fudge was not careful with his words, he didn't bother with politeness. He was always a brooding sort of fellow, wanting to get off the island and see the world. That's what I loved about him most: that he wanted a wider world. I always thought we'd travel together. But after Grem and Poppy's death, he became, dare I say, an angry person. Have you ever heard of an angry rhys dwfen?"

Carissa reflected on Sal and Toffee, the only other two rhys dwfen she'd ever known. They could be riled when the dinnerware was unpolished, or their house wasn't perfectly in order, but angry? She'd only ever seen that in Fudge.

"I can't say I've ever seen an angry one other than Fudge, but given what happened, it's completely understandable."

"Not around here—and not to the point of accusing outsiders. We're known as the friendliest fae in the world.

Mostly that's because this island has never known tragedy. We certainly had not until that accident. Ha! 'Accident,' they'd called it—couldn't even accept that it was anything more."

"So there was no investigation?"

"No, and I wasn't pushing for one either, for which I do feel guilty. But you have to understand, no one knew that Grem had given me that talisman. Of those few who knew there was a talisman, they thought Grem had buried it somewhere on the island or traded it at sea. Whatever had happened to it, they would never have connected it with me. And as long as they didn't, it and the island were safe."

"But why would whoever killed Grem and Poppy stop there? Why wouldn't they turn the whole island upside down looking for the talisman if it's so powerful?"

"Rhys dwfen might be a generous people, but don't think we don't have power, Cari. Our magic is no less than an elf or a sidhe, and because of our friendliness, we have powerful allies—no less than Tuatha de Danann like MacLir."

Carissa nodded, thinking. MacLir, Raven, Macara, and the elves and sidhe on the island might have been the only reasons the humans of Moss Hill were safe living among faeries. Powerful magic and powerful alliances might always be needed to keep the underlie at bay. But it did beg the question of how Fudge had been safe traveling on the sea away from such safe spaces.

She asked, and Raz explained, "The *Scuabtuinne* was the only boat Fudge trusted. The next time it came to port, he and Sal asked for passage to an island where Sal could grow to be himself and Fudge could meet all kinds of interesting people. Fudge thought the Rhy Dwfen would be judgmental of Sal. That's not acceptable here—to be unaccepting like he'd assumed—but Fudge couldn't see it. He became more and more convinced he and Sal would never really be part of this community.

"I blame myself for that, because whenever I looked at Fudge, I felt guilty. I knew Grem and Poppy's killers were after the talisman. I also knew that if Fudge found out I had it, he might be in danger, too. When I pulled away from him, Fudge felt that he was no longer welcome among any of the rhys dwfen. So he left."

"Where is the talisman now?" Carissa asked.

Raz rose and walked to the kitchen, waving a hand as a gesture for her to follow. Carissa kept close enough behind to watch as he opened a lower cabinet, moved aside bottles of cleaning supplies, and lifted the base panel. The cupboard floor lifted to reveal a hidden compartment. He retrieved a box therein.

Carissa took it as offered. The flawless wood craftsmanship of the container had a leprechaun's touch, and the carvings depicted rogue waves and tsunamis. The talisman inside was an almost translucent blue nautilus shell, its spiral curve tricking the eye into seeing the movement of waves. In the opening of the shell sat a pearl of an indistinguishable color. It seemed as restless as the sea itself, swirling like a storm captured in a sphere. Carissa looked at Raz with an expression of awe.

"How could something so beautiful be cursed?" Carissa asked.

"The washer woman said it would lead to a death. I didn't know whose or I wouldn't have risked it." He buried his face in his handkerchief.

Carissa frowned. She'd heard the same warning, which meant it was not Grem and Poppy's death alone that the talisman would take. If it had yet to occur, it hadn't meant Otto's death either, though in a way it had led to his death, too. No, it was "someone as good as family." Carissa cared for Sal, as she did for Tabitha, but she wouldn't consider Grem, Poppy, or Otto family.

Still, the thought of their deaths did cause a sharp pang in her chest. Carissa glared at Raz.

"You risked fate again by using the talisman now. You saw our ship through that telescope I saw in your collection, and you created the fog so that we would turn away."

Raz nodded. "In all of Sal's lifetime, I never used it until a few days ago. I have no skill with it either. I tried to surround the island so that you would avoid it. But the fog centered on your ship instead, and now it's growing, and I can't stop it. Perhaps you can try."

Carissa looked down at the pendant. The pearl seemed to pulsate with power. She felt the magic radiating from it. Putting her hand over the shell, Carissa closed her eyes and felt her Tuatha de Danann magic flowing through her as she'd done many times now. She assumed the talisman worked in much the same way—on natural instinct. She allowed the feeling of clarity and lightness to flow through her, hoping it was enough to lift the fog.

Raz, still seated, pulled back the window curtain just enough for Carissa to get a glimpse outside. It was dark, making it difficult to tell whether the sky was clearing. There was still some cloudiness to the air.

"It took time to form. It might take some time to dissipate." Raz turned back to Carissa. "I suppose you'll take the talisman now."

Carissa closed the box, placed her hand atop it, and closed her eyes. A mauve, mini-fog surrounded the box, sealing it with Carissa's Tuatha de Danann magic. "It belongs in the hands of people who can control the magic. The Tuatha de Danann could do as much."

"Yes. You're right, of course. When you take it to them, please give them my apologies for the foolish use of it."

Carissa handed the box to Raz. His mouth dropped, and his eyes questioned her. "You should be the one to deliver this to them."

"Me? Why?"

"You had this talisman all this time, and all you've thought to do with it is protect Sal. However misapplied the sentiment was, it was kindly motivated. I think you've proven you're trustworthy. Besides, we could use your knowledge on this journey."

Raz saw through her. "Ah, I see. You pity me and are trying to help me fulfill my dream of traveling. You are very kind, but I couldn't protect the talisman as well as you."

Carissa took Raz's hand and put the talisman in it. "Even before coming here, I knew that rhys dwfen magic is more powerful than the people of this island show the rest of the world. Besides, if there's a traitor looking for this talisman aboard the *Scuabtuinne*, then they'll expect this to be with me and not with you."

Raz smiled. "I see your point. Yes. Yes, I'll help you take this to Hy Brasil."

Carissa grinned, adding, "And then on to Moss Hill."

"Oh, no. How could I? I feel so filled with shame. My greed led, however inadvertently, to the deaths of Fudge's sister and brother-in-law. I couldn't face him."

"He'd forgive you. He never married. Now, I think that's because he's still in love with you," Carissa said.

Raz cried a single, solitary tear. "Even if he could forgive me, he wouldn't want an old man who, with all his big ideas, turned out to be nothing but an old bookseller with a broken-down cart whose only journeys were through stories."

Carissa placed a hand on the crook of his elbow. "You're taking a real journey now."

As Carissa stood, a noise at the window caused her to freeze. The rustling became a bang and a grunt. Raz put a shaky finger on the curtain and pulled it all the way back. Carissa shot elf-light at the window, enough to see that the fog had cleared somewhat and that a figure lay sprawled on the ground.

"Stay here," she said to Raz as she slipped the box into the inner pocket of her coat.

She yanked the door open to face the intruder. He stayed on his back, groaning with a hand to his forehead. Carissa readied her Tuatha de Danann magic. The pink mist swirling around her hands caused the man to look up. He thrust a palm out.

"No, don't! It's just me!"

"Neal?" Carissa recognized the elf but was far from putting down her defenses. "What are you doing here?"

"It's not what you think. Someone was following you."

Carissa raised an eyebrow. "Someone other than you?"

He kept his hands in the air.

"Okay, yes, I was following you, but only to make sure you were safe."

"Is that why you were on the *Scuabtuinne* tonight?"

It was a leap of logic, but something had made the talisman glow. Keeping one fist wrapped in magic, Carissa used her other hand to pull one of the two necklaces out of her shirt. The seashell pendant in her hand was dark. Carissa looked between it and Neal.

He replied almost breathlessly, "What? I haven't been on the *Scuabtuinne*. I saw someone tailing you from the inn. I wanted to make sure you were safe."

Carissa weighed his words against the talisman. It had glowed on the ship, but not now. What did that mean?

Neal stood and dusted the dirt off his knees. "I lost you turning the corner. I just arrived a minute ago and saw him listening at your window."

"And you fought him off? What type of fae was he?"

"I didn't see his face. I don't think I fought him off as much as he chose to flee. Whoever it was, his skill in combat is greater than mine." Neal touched his lip with a knuckle. It came away bloody.

The magic dimmed in Carissa's palm. He certainly looked like a fae who'd been in a fight. She couldn't continue to accuse him, though trusting him may not be the right choice either.

For good or ill, Carissa had just revealed herself to him. Yet, he didn't look surprised to see her Tuatha de Danann magic. Either he'd never seen such magic, or he somehow knew who she was already.

He could very well have made up the story about a stalker. Then again, if he had followed her alone, he'd just revealed his presence with the loud noises, and it had sounded like a fight. But if he'd fought off a stalker, who was it?

Raz appeared in the doorway. "Is everything all right?"

"Yes, but this man is injured, could we get some healing salve for his lip?" Carissa said.

"Thank you," Neal said as he walked past her into the house.

Carissa scanned the yard, but neither saw nor heard evidence of any other person. Now that the fog was lifted, she'd keep an eye out on the way back to the hotel. At the moment, she had a duty to heal a patient and to assume he was innocent of any wrongdoing. Her gut told her everyone was guilty. It only made her fear all the more for Cameron, which is why she uttered a small wish to the stars, repeating Raz's sentiment.

"Please, let everything be all right."

***

CARISSA AWOKE TO the rustling of keys in the lock. She was up and throwing on her robe before the door opened. Cameron blinked as she clicked on a light.

"Cari? I thought you'd be asleep a long time ago."

"I thought you'd be back before now, too."

"Why are you whispering?"

Carissa looked at the sprites. Cameron nodded. He walked between the two beds and yawned in the middle of an attempt to kiss her on the forehead. He sat on the mattress, running a hand through his hair.

"I'm exhausted."

Carissa sat beside him. "What happened?"

"You should've seen it, Cari. How do I even describe it? We traveled at least a mile underwater when we saw what looked like a newly sunken ship. When we descended toward the deck, dozens of water fae lined the railing and cast a magical netting over the ship. There was a gentle rush of water that radiated in a circle outward. We felt it, but it barely pushed us back. At first, I thought it might be a defense and attack, but Logan continued on as if it were nothing."

"What was it?" Carissa asked.

"Apparently, it was the fae draining the ship of water to allow us to have air to breathe on board."

"Speaking of which, how did you have air to get there? I know you said Beathan's team would take you to the water fae city, but does Beathan have ships or something for humans to travel underwater safely?"

"Yes, though not the best way. She gave us a type of seashell necklace that created an air bubble, but we basically had to be carried by the water fae. It's so weird riding a horse underwater, but especially so when you know he's also a fae who can take human form. I tried not to think about it."

"What happened when you got there?"

"First, I had to take a moment to admire the craftsmanship. Imagine the largest cruise ship you've ever seen, outclassing the *Titanic*, only it's completely underwater and sailing through the ocean like a submarine. It was a whole city of house-sized cabins and common areas. Their council chambers took up the whole center of the ship, just as breathtaking, forgive the pun, as the Sidhe Council in Vale, but it was representative of a number of different fae types. I'd say that they are more democratic than we are—there are no separate councils for different faerie people, just the one."

"What did they say about Otto and the fae we saw on board last night?"

"They denied it was them, of course. But they did agree not to accept any new water fae into their city without Logan vetting them first. If an unseelie fae is out there, they said they have an equal investment in ensuring that the unseelie do not board their ship, either."

"All that took halfway into the night to decide?" Carissa asked.

Cameron yawned again.

"We had to work out all the details, Beathan had to review their protocols, and Logan wanted to sign an official treaty between us so that they would protect Moss Hill."

"You sent a water fae city to Moss Hill?"

"They've been there before, you know. It's been about fifty years, but they didn't do any damage the last time they were there. Besides, it's interesting to think about, but I probably have some very distant cousins on board considering my heritage. I always meant to look into that. Maybe once this whole voyage is over, I can."

Carissa put a hand on Cameron's cheek to draw him out of his daydreaming.

"Cam, this is important. We won't be in Moss Hill, but an entire city of water fae, one of whom might be responsible for the death of a Mossie, will be surrounding the island while we're away. Why would Logan think that's a good idea?"

Cameron pulled her hand away and placed it between his own.

"The water fae believe something big is coming. They've been attacked more and more by unseelie pirates. They have never been infiltrated, thankfully, but they fear a large scale attack will happen soon. Based on what I told them about the events in Moss Hill this past year, they predict we're in for the same misfortune. They want to help. And we're stronger together."

The words "unseelie pirates" stuck out. Neal had never actually admitted to being a pirate, but he fit the description. Though he claimed to have fought off a mysterious stalker, he could have easily overheard her conversations with Tabitha and Hela and followed her straight to the talisman.

If he had, though, he hadn't fought her or Raz for possession of it. Perhaps the only reason Neal, or whoever the perpetrator was, hadn't killed her was because she was a Tuatha de Danann. If so, he'd have to know that her magic was still protecting the talisman, and indeed Raz's home. He'd be safe for the night, she hoped. Still, the washer woman's warning stayed fresh in her mind. Anyone who knew about the talisman might be in danger. That would include Cameron if she told him about it.

Carissa would not—no, she could not—take that chance.

Chapter 14

Ships Passing in the Night

With the fog lifted, Captain Logan decided it was once again time to set sail. They packed their bags in the morning and traveled early to board the *Scuabtuinne*. Carissa was relieved to see Raz approaching the dock with one brown bag in each hand. She walked to him the moment she saw his signature brown fedora.

"Not wearing the orange ivy cap Hela gave you?" she teased.

"I did bring it, but I think Sal found it more appealing than my simple taste can appreciate."

Carissa laughed. "They're a good group to have as traveling companions. You'll see."

"I'm looking forward to it."

A druid arrived between them to take their bags.

"Oh, wait a moment," Raz said. He pulled out a mirror from the one suitcase and then allowed the druid to continue about his work.

Carissa took the mirror in hand, recognizing it immediately.

"You stole this from our room?" She felt her jaw tightening and her trust slackening.

"You must think I'm terrible. Please, let me explain."

Raz walked farther than the gangway, toward the end of the dock where no one was standing, so that they could talk unheard. Then he continued, "I thought if you used this mirror for Sal to see who it was that killed his parents, you'd go after them. Sal would surely follow you. I'm not brave myself, but I can recognize bravery in others. That trait can get people killed. I never saw the fae responsible for Sal's parents' deaths, but if you'd seen the destruction he left in his wake, you'd understand why I don't want Sal going after a fae like that. It's not an ordinary fae who can do what that fae did."

Carissa gave a nod, half believing his excuse. "You said the beach was all torn up. But a ship crashing into the shore would have done that damage."

"No one ever saw a boat that morning, which means either the boat was a dinghy carrying only one or two people—"

"Or it was cloaked," Carissa finished.

Raz swallowed as if the thought still caused fear all these years later. "Everyone knows that the *Scuabtuinne* is the only vessel that can cloak itself because it's the only one with a Tuatha de Danann on board whose power could cloak it. Yet, the destruction was so bad on the beach; everyone thought a ship must have crashed at full speed. But if it was just one or two fae…"

"They would have had to be powerful," Carissa concluded.

Raz nodded. "After everything you told me last night, I realize I was wrong to keep things from you. I'm sorry."

"You're making up for it by being here now. I'm sure Sal will be glad to have your company," Carissa assured.

In the back of her mind, she hoped she wouldn't regret inviting Raz aboard. She no longer suspected him of Otto's or anyone else's death, but his good intentions so far had amounted to sabotage. Her worries about Raz, Otto's death, the possible presence of a saboteur on board, the safety of her friends, and the washer woman's warnings followed her as she boarded the *Scuabtuinne*. They stayed in her mind as she entered her joint cabin with Cameron. He noticed her preoccupation while unpacking the few belongings she and Cameron had taken to the inn. Deciding the return of the mirror would cause him no harm to know, Carissa explained about Raz, minus the detail of the talisman.

"I see what you mean about not trusting him, but at least he gave the mirror back," Cameron said. "If Sal can remember what he saw as a toddler, we might know what his parents' murderer looked like. I say we show it to him right away."

"I doubt I can catch Sal alone until after lunch. Hela is making it her personal responsibility to tend to Sal and Tabitha. She's barely letting those two out of her sight. She's worrying enough for both of them, and it's not good for the baby. I think it's best not to arouse her suspicions."

"I agree. Boy, I wish she'd just have stayed in Moss Hill. If I were Fen, I would've put my foot down and not allowed my pregnant wife to make such a dangerous voyage."

"Would you?" Carissa's eyebrow raised.

Cameron placed a hand on the back of his neck. "Okay, no, I don't mean you. You're stronger than Hela, obviously. I meant if she were my wife—"

Carissa's eyebrow inched higher.

"You know what I mean." Cameron cleared his throat. "You've got everything unpacked here, right? I think I'll go see what Logan is doing."

He kissed her on the cheek tentatively. She grinned as she watched him leave. She knew what he meant, not that she agreed with it, but Hela was a handful. Still, no one could discount the fact that Hela was the head elf's daughter and well trained in magic from the youngest age. She might prove herself stronger than anyone thought if she ever needed to defend herself.

Carissa decided to take a chance and see if Sal was ready to look into his past. Grabbing her newly gifted spider-silk purse, she tucked the mirror inside. The deck had the usual crew going about their business.

Carissa crossed to the stern, where Sal's room was situated. Almost directly in front of his door, she saw Ennis standing at the railing. She thought nothing of it but knocked on Sal's door. But then, Ennis called out Carissa's name. Carissa turned to see him pointing at an object roughly a hundred feet behind them. Carissa put a hand to her forehead and squinted.

"Is that one of the water fae's ships?" she asked.

Ennis's face darkened. "Pirates."

Carissa gripped the railing. She recognized the design of their mast. It was the same as a calling card given to her by a certain nosy elf.

"Do you think they're following us?" Carissa asked.

"No way to tell yet. If they do continue, the water fae will have to be alerted."

"With a Tuatha de Danann on board, I doubt they'd sneak in and attack."

He looked surprised. "Forgive me, but did the islanders know what you are?"

"No, not at all. I meant the captain."

"Ah, I see. You're thinking of the legend of Lugh. I suppose they may still think he's the captain."

Carissa's elf-ears twitched. His reaction was wrong. "Not just the legend. Lugh is still captain, even if he goes by Logan now."

Ennis let out a single chuckle. "Now I understand your confusion. Logan likes to conflate captains. No, Lugh died a century ago. Then Beathan was the captain for a while. She never really wanted the position. So, MacLir, as the original owner of the ship, appointed Logan as captain a decade ago."

"So, Logan isn't a Tuatha de Danann? What type of fae is he?"

Ennis tilted his chin curiously. "He's not a fae at all, miss. Logan is human."

Carissa's mouth dropped like an anchor. She stood like that, looking out at the pirate ship for at least a full minute. She almost didn't realize when Ennis left or when Cameron returned with the sprites.

"Brunch is on. Did you talk to Sal?"

"No, um, not yet."

"Well, should we see if he's in?"

"I knocked already. Cameron, did you know the captain has been lying to us this whole time?"

"What do you mean?" Concern creased the space between Cameron's eyebrows.

"He's human."

Cameron's face relaxed. "Does it matter?"

"Of course, it does. How can we trust him?" She pushed herself off of the railing.

Hiya and Cynth looked between the two of them and at each other. Chaos nudged Cameron's shoulder with her body. He leaned on the railing.

"I know he's human. He told me almost the first night we were on board."

Carissa stepped closer, wanting to push him herself. "Why wouldn't you tell me? And Chaos, you knew this, too, didn't you? That's why you were angry with Logan. All his stories weren't true. At least you had the right reaction. Cameron, don't you think it's important information that our captain likes to pose as a Tuatha de Danann?"

Cameron reached a hand out and tried for her hand, but caught her wrist as she tried to pull away. He held her arm gently.

"I know you're upset, and I'm sorry. But just because he's human doesn't mean he's not the right captain for this journey. Raven trusts him. I trust him. Why don't you?"

Carissa pulled away. "Why are you so fascinated by him?"

Cameron laughed. "You've known me all your life. Is it really that puzzling?"

"You think you're like the captain, but you're not."

"No, you're right, he's captain of a fae vessel, despite the fact that he's human. He doubts himself, you know. On the outside he talks like he's confident, but he wonders if the Immortal Flame will ever go out on him."

"Why would it go out?"

"It dwindles if it judges the captain to be unworthy. Self-doubt can make a person unsuited to a role they are worthy of in every other way."

Now Carissa took his hand and sat with him on the edge of the bed. "I'm still not happy he lied, but I understand why it's important to you. I keep thinking I'm protecting you." Carissa let out a solitary laugh. "Just like Raz thought he was protecting us by creating a fog. I see now that my protecting you was just fear clouding my judgment. I do trust you. I know you're capable of so much, Cam, and one day you'll know exactly what you want to do and you'll be remarkable at it."

He kissed her hand. "All I wanted was your faith in me. That, and a home with you in Moss Hill."

"Mmm," she leaned into him. "One on top of a hill, where we can see all of the island. An island of fae and human all together."

"I'd love that," Cameron said. Then he rose, holding an arm to escort Carissa to the dining hall. "For now, let's just enjoy the food and friends waiting for us, shall we?"

It was a playful deflection of a serious topic, but Carissa had had enough of grave situations in the last few days to welcome the lightheartedness. She slipped her arm around his elbow and walked with him to brunch.

***

SAL DID NOT show to the dining hall. Raz was jovial enough through the beginning of the meal that it barely gave anyone a chance to miss Sal. Even Hela seemed to be warming to Raz. But Raz himself noticed Sal's absence a few minutes into the meal. Hela responded that he had been in poor spirits since his cousins' rejection and had just asked to be alone minutes before.

Suddenly, the talisman began to glow. Carissa and Cameron glanced at each other in the same second that a scream unleashed panic in the dining hall. The nature faeries stopped prancing around the buffet tables and flew to Carissa and Cameron. Everyone seemed to stand at once and their heads all turned to the center of the ship. Carissa ran for the door to see who had uttered the cry outside.

It was Beathan. If she'd been falling into the water, she might have been saved, but she fell from the mast.

Hela and Tabitha looked to Logan, but Carissa knew he had no power to save her. She reached both hands out, and her pink mist flooded the deck. The mist cushioned her fall, sinking like a pillow around Beathan and slowly dissipating to rest her gently onto the deck. Beside her fell an orange ivy cap.

"I don't need the help. It's him," Beathan said, looking up.

"Help!" a meek voice cried from the top of the mast.

Carissa set eyes on a terrified rhys dwfen standing on the top of a sail, clinging to a wooden beam.

"Sal! Good heavens, save him, too!" Hela said.

Several druids' wands lit, standing by for orders from Logan. His attention was on Beathan. He helped her up as everyone else kept their eyes on Sal.

"He's slipping," Cameron said as Sal wobbled and held on for dear life.

"Can you catch him the way you caught me?"

Carissa's heart thumped so loudly the sound nearly drowned out Beathan's question. Although her elf-light and Tuatha de Danann magic combined in a sparkling cloud at her palms, she hadn't fully cushioned Beathan's fall. She'd survived perhaps only out of sheer luck. Carissa wasn't sure she could create a soft enough landing for Sal.

Before Carissa had time to think, Tabitha shouted with both hands curled around her mouth, "Jump, Sal! Carissa will catch you!"

Poor Sal, thankfully, was far too scared to make the leap. It gave Carissa enough time to create the same type of magical safety net for Sal to an even thicker degree. But in the center of the mist, there was a black fog forming. Carissa looked up to see Sal had just taken the plunge, but she wasn't sure she could sustain the mist long enough to catch him. Even with two hands thrust outward and the full force of her magic flowing from her palms, the darkness at the center was tearing her creation apart.

Chaos added her magic to the mix, and Hiya and Cynth flung themselves toward Sal's now panicking form. They tried to slow him with their faerie dust as he flung his limbs wildly. Between the two sprites decreasing his speed and Chaos strengthening Carissa's magic, Sal landed with less than a possible bruise on his bottom.

Sighs of relief traveled all around the group. Hela's was the loudest, escalating into tears as she threw her arms around him.

Tabitha, rather than joining in the joyous outcries, cried out, "You stop there!"

Her changeling magic roped around Beathan, lassoing the water fae in a tight grip.

"What are you doing? Release her," Logan demanded.

"You all saw it. She sabotaged the rescue, didn't she, Cari?" Tabitha asked.

All eyes turned to Carissa. The looks around the deck varied from outrage to uncertainty. Sal looked confused as Hela helped him stand. Beathan herself only eyed Carissa as if waiting for her conviction. But Carissa wasn't certain of her guilt. She'd been closest to the magic, but as far as Carissa had seen, she hadn't made a move.

"I didn't see who was behind it," Carissa said.

Tabitha only tightened the hold. Cameron stepped forward. He held a cautious hand out as he advanced.

"We can't just convict her without proof. I think it's important to hear them both out before we jump to any conclusions."

Carissa winced at the unintended pun but was grateful for the attempt.

Logan asked Sal, "What happened? Why were you up there?"

Sal's voice shook as he answered. "I...I don't know. I was walking to brunch. I was a little late, I didn't see anyone on deck, so I hurried. Then I felt like the breath had been knocked out of me, and when I came to, I was up there, surrounded by all that black mist. I didn't even know where I was. Then I felt a hand on my shoulder, I screamed, and suddenly Beathan was falling."

"Did she attack you?"

"I don't know."

Logan asked Beathan, a little gentler than he'd done with Sal, "What happened?"

Beathan stared long and hard at everyone on deck before she spoke. "I saw the black mist and left my post to investigate. I climbed the mast easily, and if I'd had my talisman, I could have saved him just as effortlessly. But it was not in my quarters when I returned to the ship this morning. I suspect whoever took it is also responsible for the mist."

To that, both Carissa and Tabitha looked at the ground. Now that she knew that it wasn't the real Talisman of Tethra, Carissa felt even more ashamed for taking it. Tabitha released Beathan and stepped back.

Since no one else knew why this testimony would convince Tabitha of Beathan's innocence, murmurs of speculation swept over the druids and water fae alike. Carissa felt another question was more imperative.

"Raz, wasn't that the green hat Hela gave you?"

Raz looked at her like the question was embarrassing. He looked to Hela, saying, "I'm sorry, it wasn't my style. I thought Sal would appreciate it more."

Hela frowned, but said to Carissa, "It's only a hat, why is that so important?"

"Because with it on, Sal might look like Raz from behind," Carissa explained.

"So, who was the attacker targeting?" Cameron asked.

"Do you think it's because of the…" Raz gulped and turned pale at the thought that someone knew he had the Talisman of Tethra.

Carissa felt a surge of fear as she raced back to the dining hall. If the attacker knew the plan for Raz to keep the talisman, they should have gone for his bags in his rooms. If they didn't know and Sal's attack had only been a distraction, they might try for the talisman in Carissa's purse. In the empty banquet hall, the bag was not where she had left it. It was traveling across the dining hall by a figure dressed as a druid with its hood up over its head.

"Stop!" Carissa shouted.

Without turning, the figure burst into a run. Carissa shot her mist at it, knocking the culprit forward just enough to stumble. She ran up and seized the side of the bag. The figure yanked it back, but without turning around, and since the material was such strong spider silk, they couldn't rip it out of her hands. He or she let go before the room filled with spectators.

Cameron was the first to run into the room. Logan, Beathan, and Tabitha followed in short succession. Soon after, Fen led a wobbly Hela and an even shakier Sal inside.

"What's wrong? Are you okay?" Cameron asked.

Carissa leaned down and picked up her bag. "It's all still here, thank goodness."

"Someone tried to steal your bag?" Logan walked past Carissa to peer out of the exit behind her. A few druids who had now entered the room received their instructions from both Beathan and Logan to chase after this unknown assailant.

With Cameron's hand on her shoulder, Carissa said, "I'm fine. It was someone dressed as a druid, but they didn't put up much of a fight. I don't think he or she wanted me to see their face."

"One of my druids, a thief?" Logan asked.

"It may not have been one of them. Raven suspected one of Niall Shae's spies had snuck on board. Cameron thought he saw the Ocean Reaper the night Otto died. It could have been him in disguise."

"But Raven said he hadn't escaped."

"Or did she?" Carissa asked. "Couldn't someone have replaced the real note for a fake one?"

Tabitha put a hand to her chin. "It was a crow that brought the note to me. If it was switched, they'd have to have power over one of Raven's crows. I don't see how that's possible."

"Couldn't it have just been any crow?" Cameron asked.

"In the middle of the sea?" Fen made a good point.

Tabitha erased all but the tiniest doubt. "I was the fae watcher of the forest. I know my creatures. I can recognize Raven's crows."

But the feeling nagged at Carissa that the thief, and possible murderer, was not a regular member of Logan's crew. Ennis confirmed that much. He came into the room, cradling a sore head.

"I'm not sure what the Ocean Reaper looks like, but it was a very corporeal person who just knocked into me at the bow."

"What were you doing at the bow?"

"Sorry, sir. The helm master agreed to teach me during my free time. I should have approved that with you."

"Never mind that now, what happened?"

"I was just going to my lesson, and honestly going to tell him about all the conundrum with mistress Beathan and master Sal, but as I was walking, a person crashed into me. He looked at me with such rage. I thought he'd kill me except that we heard footsteps running down the hall. He jumped the ship, and that's when the druids found me on the floor."

"Who was the man you saw?"

"I didn't recognize him. He was not a member of the crew, sir. I should also tell you that there was a pirate ship behind us. I think it may be following us. Perhaps the perpetrator was a member of their crew."

Carissa didn't want to believe it, but the more she thought about it, the more it made sense. They hadn't seen the pirate ship on the trip to Rhys Dwfen, but Raz's fog might have covered them. Carissa stepped forward.

"I saw the ship, too. I think Ennis might be right about the culprit being one of them."

"Captain, allow me to take a team of water fae to apprehend them," Beathan said.

Captain Logan nodded. "My best druids will accompany you."

"Wait." Carissa pulled Beathan's talisman out of the bag and held it out, saying, "I'm so sorry. We—I—took the talisman. It's a long story, one which I will gladly explain to you and the captain, along with offering my deepest apology."

"Our deepest apologies," Tabitha said.

Carissa added, "We hope you can forgive us for this transgression."

Beathan took the talisman without saying a word. Her hard-to-read expression did not ease Carissa's conscience. At least Logan didn't press Carissa to explain in front of everyone. The moment Beathan and the druids left, Carissa attempted to make amends with Logan. He waved off any need for a defense.

"No damage was done, and it was returned in the end. Let's focus on the mission. Once we capture these pirates, we'll have no further cause for delay."

"But can they capture the pirates?"

Logan smiled. "Beathan is more than she seems. And Ennis, though he's only been with us a short while, shows as much skill as a druid as the best of them. They'll have the pirates within the hour. After that, we'll reach Hy Brasil by morning."

Chapter 15
A Drop in the Ocean

Pirates always caused trouble on the high seas. At least, that's what Carissa knew from books and movies. The trouble Neal caused now was not a gruesome battle and cannon fire. The reality was that Neal and his men did not put up a fight, but the condition he'd placed for their peaceful surrender was that Neal wanted to speak with Carissa Shae immediately.

For this reason, instead of helping Sal recover the memory that might identify his parents' killer, Carissa was stuck in the brig debating prisoners. Standing opposite a partition of thick metal bars between them and their prisoners, Carissa, Cameron, Logan, Ennis, and Beathan wore stoic expressions. The nature faeries were not allowed in the bridge. Tabitha, who'd insisted on coming along, paced the tiny visitors' space, eying Neal with suspicion. The sprites had insisted on going, too, but Carissa put her foot down on that. Besides, if they'd heard him, the sprites might have been persuaded by his calm plea of innocence.

"We're here to help you," Neal said.

"Nice try, Neal, or is it Niall?" Carissa accused.

"Yes, I see the similarity in our names, but I'm not Niall Shae."

"A spy for him, then?"

"Carissa, I'm the exact person you should be trusting right now."

Carissa folded her arms. "Why's that?"

"Because Raven sent me to help you."

"How convenient, since Raven never said that to me and she's not here to verify it."

Tabitha raised a finger, meekly objecting, "She did say she'd be sending help along the way."

"She sent Beathan," Logan shrugged off her point.

Neal gripped the bars. "I have proof, or I had it. There was a note in my cabin, but your druids confiscated everything." Neal looked at Ennis accusatorily.

"We haven't found any note," Ennis insisted.

"Now that is convenient," Neal replied.

"All right." Logan put a hand up in both of their directions, saying, "Raven should be in Hy Brasil by the time of our arrival. Beathan, you keep an eye on the prisoners until then, and we'll discover the truth in the morning."

"I'm staying here too," Tabitha said.

Carissa might have worried about the prisoners' safety given the rage in Tabitha's eyes. But with Beathan there with her, Tabitha had enough sense to keep her temper under control. Carissa headed upstairs with Cameron, but her mind lingered on the prisoners in the brig.

"Do you think there's any truth to what he was saying?" Carissa asked once they were above deck again.

"I don't know. Everything points to him." Cameron wrapped an arm around Carissa as the wind picked up.

The *Scuabtuinne* was making up for lost speed, causing Carissa to feel slightly sick. She had to draw her elf-light from her heart through the rest of her body to ease her stomach. It didn't help that Gerard startled her by appearing at her side.

"Are the prisoners from that ship tied to the stern?" Gerard demanded.

"Yes, why?" Cameron asked.

"I recognize the flag. It's a man for hire, a privateer, not a pirate."

"What does that mean?" Carissa asked.

"He was hired by someone—for good or ill. But it doesn't necessarily make him evil."

"So you're saying he's not behind Otto's death? Or that he is, but someone hired him to do it?" Cameron asked.

Carissa said, "Unless he's Niall Shae pretending to be a privateer. We can't make any assumptions."

"That's my point," Gerard said. "I was not the evil person you thought I would be, which I hope I am proving with my service to this ship."

"You are. You have," Cameron reassured.

"Then perhaps you may take my advice: leave open the possibility that the man you caught is innocent."

"We would never convict him without evidence," Carissa said.

"But if he's not the culprit, that would mean there really is a traitor on board," Cameron added.

"I'll keep a watchful eye," Gerard promised.

Carissa said, "I keep wondering if they meant to target Sal. It may have been a distraction to get to the talisman in my purse, they may have been targeting Raz, or perhaps they are the same fae who killed Sal's parents and they're after him now."

"But why target Sal or Raz? And how would they know Beathan's talisman was in your purse?" Cameron asked.

"It wasn't Beathan's talisman they were after." Turning to Gerard, Carissa asked, "Could you keep an eye on Raz? We'll sit with Sal tonight, but maybe you could watch over both of them tomorrow. When we get to Hy Brasil, I don't think the Tuatha de Danann will let everyone into the king's chambers. Just in case we've caught the wrong people, I'd rather have those two protected."

Gerard nodded and stalked off.

"You trust him now?" Cameron's eyebrows raised.

"The person I saw was nowhere near Gerard's build. If he's in league with Neal, why was Gerard one of the first people to offer to catch him? And if he's with some other unseelie, why wouldn't he just let Neal take the fall?"

"Good points. But what about Raz?"

"I'll ask the nature faeries to watch over him."

"And the attacker, if he wasn't after Beathan's talisman, what was he after?"

"Not here. I'll tell you when we're in the cabin and Chaos can put a spell on the room to soundproof it."

"So I assume I should go get Sal?" Cameron asked.

Carissa nodded. "I just hope Sal is ready to discover the truth."

***

THE TRUTH WAS murky—approximately two hundred years too fuzzy to get a clear picture of it. The only thing they could see for certain was the red hair and beard. The image of a man crouching over Sal's toddler self, with the sun's glare soon covering the face, was not enough to positively identify the culprit.

"That could be anyone," Carissa said.

"He looks like a very tall version of Barnaby." Cameron squinted at the mirror.

"Could be Neal," Sal suggested.

"Except for the beard," Cameron stated.

"Beards can be shaved. I don't think that's enough to go on."

"I'm sorry," Sal said.

"You're doing well, really," Carissa praised.

Cameron said, "We'll just try again."

Sal stood, leaving the mirror on the table. "I've already tried ten times. I'm not sure I can do any better."

Carissa left her seat and headed to the door.

"Where are you going?" Cameron asked.

Opening the latch, she said, "We need Raz. He's used all sorts of odd and ancient things. He's our best chance of using this properly."

"I'll stay with Sal and the faries," Cameron said as Sal sank back in his seat. Hiya and Cynth snored from a pillow on Carissa's bed. Chaos's head dipped a few times as she sat on the table.

Once Carissa was out the door, it was evident she was not alone. In the cool night air on the deck of the ship, she was greeted by the sight of all the druids, watching the sea and waiting for something.

She would have asked what was happening, except that she saw Logan, sitting apart from all the others on the forecastle deck with a bottle of Fire Ale in his hand and his arms draped over the railing. Carissa knew she should be going straight to Raz, but curiosity compelled her to pass all the crewmen to sit beside the captain. He acknowledged her presence by raising a bottle.

"Drink?" Logan asked.

Carissa put her hand up. "What's going on?"

"Land ahead. We'll be in Hy Brasil by morning."

The night was clear, but Carissa saw no land ahead. Her gaze drifted to a blank stare ahead. Logan looked at her, then rolled his eyes.

"You want to ask me something else."

Carissa focused on him. "I know you're not Lugh. You're human. Why pretend to be Tuatha de Danann?"

"Seafaring among fae requires strength. If you're cunning, the perception of strength is enough."

"Your druids know the truth, though, don't they?"

"Very few people in this world know who I am," Logan said while staring at the open waters.

"Isn't that difficult—not being true to yourself?"

He took a drink before answering. "Truth can be painful."

"What is the truth?"

He looked at her blankly, then set the Fire Ale on the deck. "I was an orphan until I met MacLir on the day my village was destroyed by a hurricane."

"That's the same story you told in the cabin. It's Lugh's story."

"No. Not every story I told was Lugh's. That one was mine. Being captain of the *Scuabtuinne* made it easy for me to blur the lines, to forget."

"To forget what?"

"Troubles only an old sailor knows."

Logan grabbed the railing and hoisted himself up. He offered a hand to help her up.

Carissa gave a compassionate look at Logan as he lifted her to her feet.

"Oh, don't eye me with pity. It's been an adventurous life. It's what I wanted."

"It's not for everyone," Carissa said.

Logan chuckled. "Beathan didn't want it."

"She was offered the position?"

"She was temporarily assigned to the role, specifically to find me on that island. MacLir was the one who chose me, though I can't fathom why."

"You never asked him?"

Logan shrugged. "I guess it was because I was older than most of the kids in my orphanage—fifteen at the time. So, I saw it as my duty to make sure the other kids were safe. They stayed safe and calm through the whole storm. After, some were helping care for the injured, and the older children and I were helping rebuild the village by the time Beathan arrived. They were some of the best kids on the island, despite their circumstances. They were brave."

"They were brave because you were brave."

"Sounds nice, but no. They were brave because life handed them such circumstances where one was courageous or doomed. The truth is I was with them before the crisis because I had nowhere else to go, and then I left them the moment I had an out."

"You had an incredible opportunity," Carissa said.

"I have had a million opportunities, but never the chance to unite worlds. I had to leave my human life behind, lie to old friends, and accept that I would never see them again, and I never doubted the sacrifice until I heard of you."

"I made you doubt your choice to join the *Scuabtuinne*?"

"The thought of a whole world like Moss Hill made me doubt whether a sacrifice like that was ever really necessary, or if I could've been honest with my friends—essentially my family—instead of breaking ties with them."

"Maybe soon, you'll be able to see them again."

"Therein lies the difficulty about serving with the fae; I've been given life beyond my years. My friends are all gone now to old age."

"I'm sorry," Carissa said.

Logan checked the old-fashioned pocket watch in his breast pocket and showed the face to her. "It's past twelve, my dear. Sorry is for the dead of night. Hopeful is a better choice for the morning."

Carissa watched the minutes tick by with newfound hope.

"Well," a voice called out from behind them, "good morning, then!"

"Raz? I was just going to see you, but I didn't expect you to be up," Carissa said.

"Couldn't sleep. Besides, I used to love this," Raz replied.

"What, sailing? I thought you never sailed before."

"Not sailing, what you two are doing: stargazing. Fudge and I used to name the constellations, preparing for when we'd sail away. Before, you know, before everything happened."

Logan, who did not know but could suspect some hint of sadness at his tone, clapped him on the back and said, "Well, you are traveling now, my friend."

Raz beamed. "Yes, I am, and to Hy Brasil no less. Thank you both for letting me join you on this historic journey."

The genuine excitement in his expression doused the hope in Carissa's eyes. Historic, yes, but in what way? The Tuatha de Danann had already said no to helping humans and fae many times in the past, why should they say yes to her? Oh, yes, her fae, human, and Tuatha de Danann blood made her uniquely qualified to ask the question for all three races, but what about her was so worthy of getting a different answer?

She excused herself from Logan's company and asked Raz to go with her to see Sal. As soon as Raz helped them clear the image in Sal's memories, she would have to refocus her attention on her speech to the Tuatha de Danann. Somehow, her words would have to influence their hearts into action.

Logan called out to all of the passengers as he went to take over the helm, "When you come back out, be sure to use your double sight. You won't want to miss the view of Hy Brasil from the Otherworld."

Chapter 16

Havoc in Hy Brasil

Hy Brasil was everything Carissa had been expecting and more. The horn blasts announcing the ship's arrival set a hundred birds flying between this world and the Otherworld. No words did justice to the palatial cityscape. The buildings were interconnected into one made of sediment, as if it had just arisen out of the sea. A type of unfamiliar seaweed and colorful corals decorated the buildings.

The whole area smelled sweet and satiating as if the air itself were nourishing their souls. Carissa breathed in deep and exhaled with a sigh. She loved Moss Hill more than any place in the world, but if she couldn't be there, this was the best alternative she could imagine.

They settled into a shipyard at a dock seemingly designed for the *Scuabtuinne*. The nature faeries, when they came out of the room with Sal and Cameron, were eager to go exploring. Carissa shook her head firmly.

"Just Chaos. I'm sorry you two, but they probably won't let anyone but the main party into the throne room anyway."

Hiya and Cynth pouted. Chaos looked at the two sympathetically as she took a place in Carissa new green purse. The perch was lower, but Carissa imagined even more comfortable than a shoulder. Raz stepped in, placing his signature brown fedora on his head.

"We can go exploring around the island. It'll be fun."

The nature faeries perked up. Taking seats on Raz's shoulders, they looked at Carissa with saucer-wide eyes. She couldn't say no. If she did, they probably wouldn't listen anyway.

Sal yawned. "Maybe after a little nap. I'm sorry, but I'm wiped out."

Carissa worried about Sal and Raz separating. That is, until she saw Gerard, true to his word, standing a few steps from Sal. Carissa smiled. Creepy as Gerard's stalker stare was, he would protect Sal from danger. The only thing to worry about was Raz and the nature faeries wandering alone. She lifted the seashell talisman off of her neck.

"Raz, will you take this and make sure Hiya and Cynth are safe?"

She didn't add that he should make sure that the talisman was safe, too. She didn't have to. He smiled and patted his breast pocket.

"I'll keep them close to my heart at all times," he said.

Raz took the necklace and placed it around his neck. Then he and the nature faeries headed to the stairs to disembark. The captain let down the gangway. Carissa and Cameron held hands going down but found themselves instantly transported on land. They blinked, taking in the sight of a golden grass field and an archway of pearls and coral marking the entrance to the largest palace Carissa had ever seen.

A young woman, barely eighteen if she'd been human, and who knows how old as a Tuatha de Dannan, greeted them with a sagely smile through lavender eyes that spoke of years beyond counting. The woman's white gown and black hair swayed in the breeze as she approached. Carissa turned to face the shore, finding that the *Scuabtuinne* was still glistening in the shipyard. Turning back to the woman, she heard the introduction.

"Welcome, travelers, we have anticipated your arrival. I will escort you to the waiting hall where breakfast will be served."

They followed the woman to a garden of the largest berries, fruit, and vegetables they had ever seen. Everything was ripe and ready for the taking. For seating, there were finely carved wood chairs and long banquet tables boasting thin gold sheets for tablecloths. Carissa would not have believed this was a "hall," except that Sal bumped into a wall and had to use his hands to find the open doorway they'd gone through. The ceiling and walls were made of some material more transparent than glass. It must have been a beauty to stand inside when it rained.

Once they were seated, Logan said, "Thank you, and will the king be joining us?"

"You will join him when you are ready to hear his answer."

"We haven't asked our question," Cameron said.

"There's no need to ask. He knows it already." The woman bowed and took her leave, disappearing behind the foliage on the other side of the wall.

"Sounds like he made up his mind already," Cameron said.

Logan replied, "If he has, it won't be in our favor."

***

WHEN KING NUADA finally called for them, the day was approaching noon. Hela had eaten heartily of the enchanted foods, as had been her plan, and was now wobbling with less than her usual elfish grace as the woman escorted them. They past a hall that seemed to be made of mother of pearl, and the treasure at the center was the Hall of Kings. The king's chair, as the Tuatha de Danann were loathed to call it a throne, sat in the center of a number of other gold- and silver-backed chairs with firm cushioning. While those chairs were raised on a platform to an exalted status, the chairs on the floor facing them offered cushions that were just as soft to the touch as Carissa imagined the royals' chairs felt when seated. In the seats facing the king, they found one occupied.

"Raven!" Carissa reached instinctively for a hug. Chaos did the same with Raven's cheek.

Raven tapped Carissa's back thrice gently. "Goodness, the two of you. Remember where we are, my dears."

Carissa let go, blushing. She'd forgotten herself in the moment, but Raven was too controlled to lose composure, even when comforting Tabitha.

Tabitha's eyes welled, and Raven held out a hand to her and squeezed her fingers. The gesture was enough. King Nuada could not be kept waiting.

Raven held a hand toward the open row of seats. Logan, Hela, Fen, and Cameron piled into the seats. Carissa went to take hers. Raven stopped her.

"Your moment of truth," Raven whispered, then she took her seat.

Carissa stood steps away from the platform, face to face with King Nuada had he not been two feet off the ground. She bowed. Nuada's voice boomed through the hall.

"There's no formality here. Any one of you may speak."

Fen stood. "Sir, since we are here to judge whether Moss Hill has succeeded in uniting humans and fae, I am prepared to recite an oral history of the island."

Nuada put a hand up. "Before you speak further, I should inform you that we watch the world. We know about Moss Hill, we heard MacLir when he came a few months past. At Raven's request, we will hear you, too. But our answer remains the same: we must stay out of the affairs of the human and fae worlds."

Fen took his seat. Hela held his hand, reassuringly. But it wasn't a good start.

Carissa raised her head high in direct contrast to her sinking hopes. "If you are certain there's nothing I can say to change your minds, then, I'm sorry, sir, that may be hearing, but it isn't truly listening."

Her muscles tensed, waiting for the backlash. Instead, Nuada's lips pulled back in a condescending smile, as if he found her response amusing. The look was shared among each royal person on the platform.

"You will say, 'It's time to unite the worlds as they have been in Moss Hill.' We will say, 'We have united the worlds before—the strong destroyed the weak, and the world Maeb wanted will come to pass.' You will say, 'Moss Hill is a successful experiment.' We will say, 'The unseelie were able to easily manipulate you, to get you to suspect and distrust each other. There have been murders on your island. We have seen it through our windows.'"

"I will say that you are so far removed from the world that you can't feel the love and friendship we have for each other in Moss Hill. Did we suspect each other? Yes, but only because the unseelie planted seeds of doubt. People were scared, it's only natural, but we also found the real culprits in the end, every time." This was her opportunity to begin the speech she'd prepared. "My grandfather's vision was to create a single town where humans and fae do not live on separate sides of an island, but in the same neighborhoods. When he died, his hopes were not realized. Vale and Moss Hill lived in peace, but separately. But just enough of the original vision lived on in us that when the unseelie came, instead of dividing us, they strengthened our bonds. More and more fae are moving into town, more and more humans are welcome into Vale. The unseelie proved that we are ready to fulfill the purpose of Moss Hill. And we are ready to lead the merging of human and fae worlds by example."

"And what of the unseelie? Where are they in this merging? Are they needed to bring you together to band against them? You plan to strengthen your human and fae bonds by fighting them off?"

"We hoped for your help to protect Moss Hill until our island is revealed to the rest of the world. The unseelie threaten the world Moss Hill is trying to create—"

"And it's a beautiful world you plan to build, but it's not the world that will be created. Each battle you win with the unseelie will inch you closer to losing the war. They'll plant seeds of suspicion that will grow into fear and hatred, and soon fae and humans will be at war again. If suspicion is natural, as you said, then it's in your nature to continue to fight," Nuada said.

Carissa stepped close enough to the podium that she could put her hands on the floor where they were sitting. She leaned over it. Overcome with passion, she said, "That's just my point. We suspect what we don't know. The more we learn about each other, the less we'll doubt each other. Our trust will grow. It takes time, but it can happen. It's happening now. If my grandfather had lived, we might be closer, but I'm here before you as a human, a fae, and a Tuatha de Danann to tell you that we're ready to move on. Wasn't that the stipulation? You told MacLir when he was here months ago that you needed all races represented before you, pleading the case that the Moss Hill experiment was a success and that you should keep the portals open between the Otherworld and the human one, and that we'll reveal ourselves to the rest of the world. Well, I'm telling you, we're ready."

Nuada looked at Raven. "You misunderstood our stipulation. One race is missing."

Carissa looked to Raven. A missing race? Raven shook her head.

"You know that's not possible. Don't be stubborn, Nuada."

Carissa's eyes darted between the two. "What's not possible?"

Nuada said, "It's not possible to bring back a group of people who are gone from the face of the earth."

Raven stood. "The Fomorians were dangerous. They threatened everyone."

One of the royals in the back matched Raven's tone. He pointed a finger at her, commanding, "Sit back and respect the king's words."

Carissa had never seen Raven do as she was told. She reminded Carissa of Chaos as she folded her arms and held her head up high as if daring the council to command her again. In fact, Chaos on Raven's shoulder copied every move. Chaos's looked transformed to surprise as Logan leaned over to whisper something in Raven's ear. Raven nodded, and Chaos flew from her shoulder out of the council chambers.

The hair raised on Carissa's neck. She wished she knew where Chaos was going, but even more so, she wanted to understand what Nuada was saying. Apparently, the Fomorians had a history with the Tuatha de Danann that no one was saying aloud.

"What happened between you and the Fomorians?" Carissa asked.

"The same thing that will happen between humans and fae."

"If the unseelie have their way, you mean," Carissa said.

"Unseelie, seelie, whoever wins, it all ends the same way."

Carissa's face twisted in fear, but she asked the question anyway, "How does it end?"

The royal family sat silently. Their thrones in blinding rays of sunlight seemed to be shouting the obvious. They were responsible for something—they were seated on precious metals, clothed in jewels and covered in shame.

Cameron rephrased Carissa's question, "How did it end for the Fomorians?"

Nuada's eyes met his, then Carissa's, and then the reflections on the gold-covered walls.

He said, "It ended at our hands: there are no more Fomorians."

The slamming of the door begged to differ. All eyes turned to see Beathan enter.

Tuatha de Danann eyes followed her as she approached. She did not bow, nor make any gesture of respect. Instead, she turned to Logan, who put a hand out to stop her from advancing. He stepped out of the row to join her in facing the king.

Logan bowed his head. "Sirs, allow me to introduce Beathan, the previous captain of the *Scuabtuinne*."

Beathan leaned in and whispered into Logan's ear, "That was not supposed to be spoken of."

Logan put a reassuring hand on her shoulder. Then he said to the king, "Please, hear her testimony before you make your final decision."

"Does she have knowledge relevant to this case?" The king seemed annoyed for the breach in protocol, even if he had said they didn't stand on ceremony.

"I think you'll find Beathan exactly what you were asking to see." He turned to Beathan, saying, "Go ahead, show them who you are."

She hesitated, her eyes pinned on Logan with uncertainty. Logan nodded. Beathan slowly turned her hands outward, and a subtle blue force field enveloped her entire body. She seemed to grow in stature, quite literally, and her hair changed from the blue-black of a water fae to the bright, fiery red of....

Carissa was lost for the word. She'd never seen anyone like her.

"A Fomorian," Nuada half-whispered. He, Raven, and every Tuatha de Danann sat on the edges of their seats.

"I am Beathan, daughter of Tethra, whom the humans call the goddess of the sea. I am one of the last Fomorians on this earth. I walk between the Otherworld, the human world, and the world beyond, with no place left for my people."

"We welcome you, Beathan, daughter of Tethra, and we grieve with you for your loss."

"Do you?" she asked.

Nuada's head hung low. His voice deepened as he replied, "For penance to your kind, we have vowed to keep away from the world. We are asked to join in helping it again but wish not to harm any as we once harmed you. Tell us what you think of this matter. We will hear you." He looked at Carissa, adding, "And we will listen."

Beathan, with her shoulders back, her chin high, and her height surpassing everyone in the room, said, "I have sailed with a human captain for many years, and though I trusted him, I still did not trust humans. I thought of him as an exception among men. But, now I have met more humans." She pointed at Carissa. "This human stole from me."

Carissa's heart froze, her eyes stung, and she found it hard to breathe. She thought for certain the vote was against her, and the whole commission doomed. But Beathan's eyes softened. "And she saved my life and returned what was taken." Pointing at Cameron, Beathan said, "And this one spoke for me when he thought I was in danger. I find my hope restored that I might live among friends again. Perhaps the Fomorians, too, can find a home in Moss Hill. Once again, the fate of a Fomorian is in your hands. What will you do with it?"

The wizened, old woman behind King Nuada cackled. For the first time, she spoke, "This is the prophecy. All races have stood represented before the council, and they all ask the same thing. This is it. The new world has begun!" Her laughter so offset the gravity of the others' expressions, that even the little joy she showed manifested like a mad woman's hysterics.

Nuada put a hand to his chin as if taking the woman seriously after all. After a soul-searching stretch of time, he nodded.

"The eldest among us is right. She knows the prophecy best. We are duty-bound to help you. We will open a window to Moss Hill to look upon this land you wish to protect. Then we will decide how best to intervene. But know this, we will strike down the unseelie once and once only. Then we withdraw to our world again."

"Not all of us." Raven rose from the chair again.

Nuada put a hand to his temple, revealing that his hand was not gloved, but a metal prosthetic. Every gut-wrenching year of his life showed in the creases of his eyes as he said, "The Tuatha de Danann do not belong in their worlds."

Raven stood her ground. "You gave your conditions. I give mine. MacLir, Macara, and myself: we all stay."

Nuada dropped his hand to the chair's arm. "Then you cannot return here ever again."

"Fine." She waved a hand as if saying no to pickles on a sandwich.

Carissa looked at her with brows creased over her concerned filled eyes, but Raven only blinked. Her cheeky grin was mimicked on Chaos's face. Carissa smiled back, but her eyes still watched them with a tinge of sadness. They were sacrificing their home for Moss Hill's, and for earth's, future.

As the hall emptied, Beathan stayed to discuss "old grievances," as Raven called them.

Raven said, "They'll punish themselves for another thousand years and then perhaps, if the world is different, they'll finally rejoin it."

"Did they really wipe out the Fomorians?" Carissa asked.

Raven attempted to hand Chaos back to Carissa. Chaos kicked and swatted her fingers. Raven continued while Chaos chimed in her ear. "It was a long war, and I had my hand in it, too. The Fomorians, the fae, and the humans: there wasn't one type of being unaffected by the fighting. The Fomorians suffered the worst, of course, the fae receded to the Otherworld, and the humans took their realm and created their kingdoms. And the Tuatha de Danann stayed away from everything, secluded on an island at the top of the world."

"Were the Fomorians as great as the Tuatha de Danann?" Carissa recalled Beathan's power and how she grew to a giant's size in the King's Hall.

"The Fomorians were as terrible. They were vicious, conniving, and unforgiving."

"You don't seem sorry for their loss," Cameron noted.

"I'm not unhappy to know that some survived. But war is war." She stopped. "There's no soldier who comes out of a battlefield feeling as innocent as a baby. But there is a difference between those who go in to fight their enemies and those who go in to protect their friends."

"Which were you?" Cameron asked. He'd gotten bolder speaking to a Tuatha de Danann this way.

"I was a general. I had to be both." Raven resumed walking. "But tell me, what is this Chaos is telling me about pirates being held prisoner on the *Scuabtuinne*?"

Chapter 17

Turning the Tide

The window was the mirror resting along the whole sidewall where the royals sat. King Nuada simply pulled back the curtain with a wave of his hand. The old woman limped down the steps without the use of a cane. Cameron leapt to assist her, but she slapped his hand away. At the mirror, she stopped and rubbed her hands together as if generating heat. Electricity gathered around her fingers, then a dark blue mist like a mini-storm. She placed both magically-charged hands on the glass. An explosion of color rippled up and down the mirror, focusing eventually on an island: Moss Hill.

The woman stepped back, staring at the sea to the east of the island. The image closed in on the water. If ever she'd seen a pirate ship, Carissa recognized the dozens racing to the shoreline.

The view changed. They floated over the streets until the woman's hands clapped the glass and the mirror shook. She thrust her arms out as if throwing the image to Carissa and the others. Suddenly, the scene enveloped everything and everyone.

Carissa turned around in awe of the fact that she and the others were now standing on a street all the travelers could recognize.

"Are we in Moss Hill?" Cameron touched the red brick wall beside the door to the Second Street Pub. His hand went through.

"Don't be silly," Raven said. "It's just a window into your world. We're just seeing what's happening there now."

"Think of a hologram." Logan's eyes caught a shadow and stared.

Carissa noticed it too: magic. Fae were using their powers in blurs of mist, light, cloud, and shadow, depending on their particular background, out in the open. The hologram zoomed from street to street. Familiar and unfamiliar faces twisted in rage.

"Get out of my shop!"

"Back off, you thief!"

"Scoundrel!"

One by one, voices compounded on each other until it seemed the whole island was talking at once. Carissa's elf-ears rang. She clamped her hands over them. Hela sunk to her knees and Fen struggled to help his wife. The others winced, though only the elves were so affected. Cameron's fingers pressed over Carissa's, yet she could still hear him shouting, "Can't you lower the sound?"

The old woman pulled her arms together and apart like a conductor at the end of a musical score. Carissa removed her hands, though Cameron's arms still lingered at her shoulders. Chaos helped Hela up by pulling her hand with her faerie dust magic.

"What's happening? Why are they all so angry?" Carissa asked.

"The seeds of discord. And you said that Moss Hill was a peaceful coexistence of humans and all sorts of fae? It doesn't look so to me," Nuada, who hadn't come off his throne to properly see the sights, lifted his chin and turned his nose away so that he couldn't see what was becoming so clear to Carissa.

"It's the unseelie. Don't you see? Mossies would never act like this. There are unseelie I've never seen before all over the area affecting them."

"Bringing out their prejudices," Nuada said.

"No, their fears," Cameron countered. "They're afraid. They feel threatened, but they don't know what they are fighting. Look closely. They're not attacking their friends and neighbors—they're not attacking at all. They're defending themselves."

"We have to help them," Hela said through tears.

Her husband finished her thought. "They can't fight the unseelie alone. Please do something."

Nuada considered the scene by stroking his chin and staring at the Mossies outside their shops and homes throwing magic and punches at giggling, threatening, shouting unseelie invaders. Goblins, bogarts, hags, pixies, and more attacked mainly humans, though they ransacked fae shops and tore up their homes with their magic. Chaos cried to see it.

Carissa understood how she felt. Her body enflamed with fae light and Tuatha de Danann magic all at once. She'd never felt so powerful before, nor so helpless.

"Do something," she practically commanded Nuada.

Beathan stood with Carissa. "Honor your promise," she said to the king.

Nuada bent his head, acknowledging his vow. Every one of the royals struck the arms of their chairs in unison. From their hands emanated a singular wave of magic from one shore of Moss Hill to the other.

The tides literally turned, rushing faster than any unseelie kelpies could run. The waves were not water, or Carissa would have worried that the whole town would drown. Instead, it was a wave of white mist—a mix of many colors of Tuatha de Danann magic so seamlessly intertwined it looked like pure light.

It rushed over all the panicky arguing people, and one by one each fell to the ground in slow motion, as if gently carried to their sleep.

Nuada said, "The sleeping spell will last one day, no more, no less. They'll be safe until your arrival, where you may sort out seelie from unseelie. This is the most we can do for Moss Hill. But as to the links between the Otherworld and the human realm, they will remain open. All links will remain but the one to Hy Brasil. We give the power over the portals between all worlds over to you. Carissa bring your hands to mine."

Carissa stepped toward the platform and walked up the steps. She placed her hands palm-to-palm with the king's. A cloud of colors mixed around their hands. Carissa felt a burst of energy run through her.

"You control the portals now. The binding is complete. Now, return to Moss Hill."

Cameron stepped forward, "We thank you, sir, but we're more than a day's journey from Moss Hill."

"Still thinking like a human," Logan said. This merited chuckles from several of the Tuatha de Danann, and the old woman hooted as if Cameron's dumbfounded expression was the highlight of her year.

When they'd all had enough amusement at Cameron's expense—and Carissa's, too, since she was likewise confused at the idea of traveling a two week's journey in a day—Logan explained, "The *Scuabtuinne* is capable of speeds that we don't often use out of respect for the ocean, but we can travel the whole of the globe in a day if we so chose."

"Besides that, the water fae city should be there within the hour," Beathan said.

"The only problem is they won't know who to cure of the sleeping spell and who to capture. We mustn't waste a moment. Let's go." Raven stomped out of the room before anyone else had taken a single step.

***

RAVEN DID NOT stop until she'd reached the brig. Carissa and Cameron could barely keep up. When they finally reached the entrance, Carissa called out to Chaos.

"You know Logan doesn't like sprites in his brig. Go make sure Hiya and Cynth are all right. No argument. If Neal isn't the attacker, Raz or Sal could be in trouble. Go!"

Instead of continuing her protest, Chaos stopped, seemed to think about her reasoning, and agreed by saluting before flying away. Carissa and Cameron walked inside the darkened cell to see Raven standing inches from the metal bars. She walked back and forth, keeping her eyes on the prisoners. Cameron gasped as the magically infused metal ceased to exist with a snap of her fingers. A very confused Tabitha opened and closed her mouth in disbelief.

Neal sat up from the straw that served as a bed and breathed a sigh of relief. "Raven, thank god."

"It's goddess. And what were you doing that got you captured?"

"Following your orders."

"I don't recall ordering you to get captured."

Carissa stepped into Raven's line of sight to glance between her and Neal. "So, you did hire him?"

"To find a spy of Niall Shae and a talisman that might protect all of you."

Tabitha unfroze. "I thought I was supposed to find the spy?"

Raven rolled her eyes. "You captured the wrong spy." She glanced at Neal and put her head in her hands. "Do please get up. Trust a fae to do a Tuatha de Danann's job? Cameron could do better than you."

"What's that supposed to mean?" Cameron said.

"Oh, sorry, dear, didn't realize you were in the room."

The offended look did not easily leave Cameron's face. Carissa put a hand on his forearm to comfort him and turned to Raven.

"So if Neal's not Niall's spy, who is?"

"Who indeed?" Raven asked.

"I've got a few ideas," Neal said darkly. "That Ennis fellow was particularly horrid."

"Beathan wasn't a peach either, was she?" one of Neal's men asked.

"I wasn't too fond of Captain Logan." The second crewmate said *"captain"* like it was a joke. The chortles around him proved the others thought it was funny. One look from Neal provoked silence from them all.

The ship jolted. Everyone stumbled except Raven. Tabitha held onto the wall, Cameron held Carissa firmly at her waist and gave a sharp, confused look to Neal as he sprung forward to help her as well. He backed down with his hands up, digressing to Cameron's role as a boyfriend. Carissa pretended she saw nothing.

She said, "I'm assuming that's Logan putting the *Scuabtuinne* into its fastest pace."

"We need to find that spy," Raven said as she paced about the room.

Tabitha joined her pacing. In the tight space of the brig, two people striding around the room was dizzying. Carissa blocked Raven's path.

"What made you think there was a spy on board in the first place?"

Raven waved her fingers dismissively. "Logan suspected that someone went through his quarters. Several crew members stated their possessions appeared to have been searched. I sent Beathan to help him a while ago, but even she had no idea who it was."

"Did you know she was Fomorian?" Carissa asked.

Tabitha's eyes widened, and she stopped pacing long enough to put her arms around Carissa and Raven. "Beathan is a Fomorian? I always miss the important details!"

Shrugging Tabitha's hand off, Raven said, "No, I didn't know. I suspect MacLir must have, though. I'll have to have a chat with him when I next see him. That's not the important part now. For the first time, I'm a bit lost on what to do. I need a moment to think."

"If only we had some clue!" Tabitha said.

"We do." Cameron stepped up. All eyes turned to him. He looked to Carissa. "The mirror."

Carissa nodded. "Otto was investigating Sal's parents' deaths. We were beginning to suspect that whoever killed his parents may have also killed Otto to protect their secret." She explained everything about the mirror, their inability to retrieve the full memory, and even Raz's failed attempt to help them clarify the image in the mirror.

"The washer woman! Of all the dangerous, foolhardy, inexplicable things for a fae to do." Raven wagged her finger.

Cameron shifted the blame, confessing, "It was my idea."

Raven turned on him. "Of course, it was. Only a human would not know to avoid the washer woman." She smiled. "And only a human of the highest order would risk self and safety for a noble cause. Now, where is this mirror? It's time we catch our culprit."

Chapter 18

Hela and High Water

The moment they climbed up to the main deck from the brig, Carissa gasped. Night had not yet fallen, but the sky was a deep, dark blue. Tabitha twirled at the sight. It wasn't often one looked up to see schools of fish swimming in a backdrop of stars. The moon floated farther up, and a cloud of jellyfish lit in its place. Tabitha couldn't help herself, reaching a hand over the railing. Her fingers glided through the water.

"Amazing, isn't it?" Cameron draped an arm around Carissa.

"I take it you've never traveled underwater before?" Neal dodged Tabitha's splashing.

"Are we forgetting why we're here?" Raven tapped an impatient foot.

"Sorry," Carissa said, moving ahead of them.

They found Gerard standing like a sentinel at Sal's door. Carissa and Cameron looked at each other. Neither had asked Gerard to guard the door, yet he did not move until he saw them. Then he uncrossed his arms and stepped aside.

"All is well. No one has entered or exited."

"Um…thanks. That will be all," Cameron said.

Raven pushed her way through first, saying, "Are you holding him prisoner?"

Sal thrust his hands in the air and leapt from the seat at the table. "Finally! That brute hasn't let me out all day. Something about you saying I needed watching over?"

"I may have said that yesterday." Carissa winced.

"Have you eaten?"

"Yes, he brought me food. But you said the Tuatha de Danann would allow us to see some of the island, and I've been cooped up here the whole time. Raz even tried to visit, but that brute just told him to go away."

"But why?" Tabitha asked.

"He may have taken me too literally. I'm sorry," Carissa said.

Sal said, "So am I, because whatever Raz wanted to tell me, it sounded important."

Carissa wondered if she should mention the talisman. Though, the chances were that he wouldn't have gone to Sal on that matter. Perhaps he'd found a way for the mirror to work. Or maybe he'd discovered the culprit himself?

"I hope he's not in trouble," Carissa said aloud.

Raven twisted her torso, looking back at Neal and his men. "Go with that kelpie and check on the rhys dwfen, will you?"

Neal bowed and set off with his men. The rest of the bunch crowded around the table on which the mirror lay.

Carissa said, "Sal, I think we're close to finding our culprit. Would you try the mirror again?"

Sal lifted the glass from the table and scratched his forehead as he sat.

"I tried it several times today, as there's nothing else to do, but I just can't get it."

"You didn't have me." Raven folded the bottoms of her sleeves.

Her hands on the glass had the same effect as the old woman in Nuada's hall. Her cloud of purple magic lit the mirror, and she handed it back. This time, Sal barely touched it, but the light nearly blinded them as the image looking back at them changed.

The red hair and beard, the brown eyes, the hood, and every feature on his face came into focus. Everything, in fact, became crystal clear.

"Hey, that's the druid who was asking me questions about Moss Hill. I spoke with him several times while we were on board." Cameron looked incredulous and his brows twisted in fear that he may have given away too much information about the town they were supposed to protect.

What worried Carissa more was that Raven's magic took the killer's image and followed him from past to present. The image zoomed to right now, this very minute, to where a new victim was confronting the villain all on his own.

"Oh no, Raz! He must've found out Raz had the talisman." Carissa would have explained more if there were more time. In the mirror, the nature faeries put up a brilliant fight but were easily swatted away. Raz tried to summon his magic but was lifted a foot off the ground and held just above the railing outside the dining hall.

"He'll be killed," Tabitha screeched.

Cameron swung the door open, and Tabitha ran through it. Raven disappeared in a puff of smoke. Carissa, who hadn't mastered that ability, followed behind Tabitha.

They reached the deck at the same time Neal's men came around the corner. Neal drew his sword.

"Look out!" he shouted as he slid to the right of Cameron and caught a water fae in the abs.

Cameron swirled around and Carissa gripped his shoulder. Water splashed over all sides of the ship as dozens of webbed hands clamored up to the deck. Fae with fins, gills, and terrible, glowing eyes appeared over the rails. The nature faeries were up and ready for the fight, but brave as they were, there were too many.

"We were being followed by water fae," Cameron said.

"They're not Beathan's fae. I don't recognize any of them," Carissa said.

"Now's not the time for realization," Neal said. "Can you fight?"

"Give me a sword, and I'll try." Cameron reached out as Neal tossed a hilt in his direction.

"Do you see Raven?" Tabitha thrust a hand out and lashed her magic like a whip against two lizard-like fae who had just made it on deck.

"There," Cameron said as he blocked a fae's scaly arm with his blade.

Carissa got the fae off with a blast of elf-light. As soon as he was free, Cameron pointed to the doors of the mess hall.

There was Raven, generating a whirlwind of magic so strong it knocked seven fae onto their backsides and slid them into the room.

Paces away, Raz struggled against some unseen force as if something were choking him on the railing. Carissa's eyes darted until she saw his attacker in the shadows.

She dashed into danger and sent a flurry of mauve-colored magic to make the shadowy figure stumble. Raz coughed. The figure regained his footing and faced her.

Carissa shouted, "Give up. We have you outmatched."

"Do you?" he goaded just as Carissa reached Raz.

Raz's eyes caught hers, and he looked down. At first, Carissa thought he was looking at the peril awaiting him if he'd fallen from the deck to the ocean below, but then she saw the varied colors of magic exploding like fireworks in the water. All of Beathan's fae were at war with the incoming onslaught.

The distraction was enough that magic was hurtling toward Carissa's face before she could stop it. Chaos, thankfully, parried with faerie dust. But it was Beathan who appeared around the corner and launched an assault of wind and water that thrust the attacker away.

Carissa had to shield her eyes with her forearms to catch a glimpse of a druid hanging onto the door of the mess hall for dear life. Yet, the druid was strong enough to create a barrier of mist-like magic around himself. It was enough to lift him to his feet and allow for his escape into the mess hall.

Not only did Carissa panic that he might be getting away, but Sal's voice shouted over the din, "Stop him! Cari, Hela's room is on the other side!"

Carissa ran as fast as her feet could travel. She prayed that the bow of the ship and the cabins there were unaffected, but there was no way to tell until she was inside the room.

Then, by the sheer number of druids both inside and visibly running toward the fighting outside the window, it was clear that the bow was filled with men readying for a fight. Logan stood in the center of them all, looking impressive despite his lack of magic, in a fighting stance and a shield of nearly translucent magic emanating from a talisman around his neck.

Though the unseelie fae were outnumbered, they laughed as they surrounded the group. Even Raven stood defensively, awaiting their next move instead of leading an offensive. The lights flickered, and a black mist rose to the ankles of every fae and druid entering the room.

Carissa acknowledged the leader, "Ennis, or rather N.S., as in Niall Shae? Look around you. Two Tuatha de Danann, a Fomorian, and a room full of fae, druids, and humans have banded against you. You can't win."

Ennis spat back, "An old has-been sea goddess, one and a half Tuatha de Danann, and a human posing as one—that's what I see. And your druids are only human. My fae aren't exactly quaking in their scales."

Low, raspy chuckles rippled through the unseelie fae.

"If you have so low an opinion of humans, why use the human surname 'Shae'?"

"My cousin, your late father, used the name. We're blood. I thought why not use it, too?"

"Don't you see? If you truly hated humans, you wouldn't have used the name."

"Camouflage. I use what I have to in order to survive."

"I don't think so. I think you used it because you cared about him, about me, about family."

"I do care about you, dear cousin. You're welcome on my side."

"I'm part-human, Niall."

"It's unfortunate, but even I have some elf-blood in me. All those fae mixing impurities can be forgiven. We'll sort them out in the Otherworld."

"Impurity? Why is your elf-blood the impurity and not your Tuatha de Danann blood? Is it because elves are lesser than you?"

"Save it. I know what you're trying to do. But we all know Tuatha de Danann magic is superior to elf-light. You won't find the unseelie turning against each other or me. They know I'm only speaking the truth."

"Are you, though? You've never seen the Tuatha de Danann on earth. No one has. Have you ever thought about why?"

"They don't dare mix with lesser magic."

"No, it's because they nearly tore the world apart with their magic! It's not superior; it's just destructive."

"Unless you know what to do with it."

"Exactly. And until the Tuatha de Danann figure that out, they won't mix with any unseelie." Carissa looked each unseelie fae in the eye. "They won't acknowledge any of you in their society."

"Who said we want to be part of their society?" said one of the unseelie in the crowd. The rest cheered.

"See?" Ennis said. "We're creating our own society. Unless you join us, I'm sorry to say, you won't be around to see it."

Chapter 19

Man of War

Raven wasn't having it. The picture of annoyance, she waved a hand as if dismissing him. Only, her simple gesture threw a translucent wave in his direction.

"Enough," she said.

Carissa traced the disturbance Raven created as it traveled through the air with enough force to push Ennis's men to the floor and halfway across the room. But Ennis remained standing. Something at his neck glowed.

"I'm sorry, Cari. He took the talisman," Raz said.

Raven shot blast after blast in his direction, but he was a Tuatha de Danann, too. And with the talisman, his power was amplified.

Carissa used her magic in tandem with Raven. The shield of the talisman held, but it was breaking. As if it were a glass shield, the magic formed cracks at the center. The light emanating from the talisman flickered.

Ennis's thugs would not let the attack continue. They ceased their attacks on Beathan and focused their attentions on Carissa. All Carissa could do was use her elf-light to quickly deflect blades that were slashing in her direction. Raven continued to exchange blasts with Ennis until he shouted with a fury that enveloped the whole room. Two streams of magic, the black mist of his Tuatha de Danann force and the celestial blue beam of the talisman, concentrated into a fine point aimed straight at Raven's heart.

"Move!" Logan crashed into Neal, who had been fending off a fae directly behind Raven.

If he had not knocked down the elf and his fae competitor, they would have been struck by the blast. It was strong enough to blast a hole right through the wall. Raven was nowhere in sight.

"Raven?" Carissa choked on her wavering voice.

"Is she...dead?"

The cawing of a crow answered Cameron. The bird flapped its wings and found shelter on a wooden beam directly over Logan's head.

"She's transformed. She'll take some time to shift her shape again."

The fight resumed. It was interrupted seconds later when double doors on the bow side shot open. Hela, in a full-length floral nightgown and robe, stood with her glowing hands held out in front of her. The clanging of swords ceased.

Hela's elf-light lifted the metal to midair, then threw them to the walls of the room. A cacophony of clashing metal reverberated. All eyes focused on the source of the magic that had scattered them.

Hela rubbed her baby bump and sternly chided the combatants, "My child is sleeping. Will you please stop practicing your swordplay for one night and let us rest?"

She didn't understand what was going on. Logan had held enough nights of sword fighting for her to think this was just another practice session. Fen understood well enough to step in front of his wife. Ennis opened his mouth wide, and a laugh erupted that soon spread among all his men. The crinkle at his eyes showed his mirth and his age. Not recognizing him, Hela placed a hand on either hip.

"Do you think sleep deprivation is funny?"

"Hela, stop." Fen put an arm behind him, keeping her back.

Ennis indulged her with a bow. "No, my lady, I wouldn't dream of denying you a long, deep slumber." The amusement in his eyes morphed to threat.

Fen turned and put both hands on her shoulders. The urgency in his voice grew, "Love, go back to bed."

Confusion fell over Hela's expression.

"What's going on?" she asked.

"Go," Fen gently urged, but Hela pushed back.

"I demand to know what is happening."

For the first time in all the years Carissa had known him, Fen used a sharp tone with his wife, "Go back to the room. Now!"

A startled Hela stepped back, blinking. Ennis put a foot forward. He reached his hand out, allowing a black mist to swirl. His other hand gripped his sword.

Hela stopped her protest long enough to catch Carissa's eyes. Carissa focused on the talisman at the collar of Neal's shirt. Awareness finally dawned on Hela's face.

Ennis walked toward Fen and Hela. "Now, Fen, we wouldn't want to be rude to Head Elf Rolin's daughter. I will tell you what is happening, my lady. We've been invited to a very special event aboard the *Scuabtuinne* tonight: your collective funerals. We'd have saved you a front-row seat, but that's been reserved for the Tuatha de Danann who was kind enough to invite us."

He made a show of bowing in Carissa's direction. The talisman hung completely outside his shirt. Hela took this as an opportunity. She slapped Ennis with one hand and reached for the necklace with the other. Ennis caught her hand just as Sal crashed into him.

"Leave her alone!" Sal shouted.

It was enough to allow Hela to wriggle free of his grasp. She clutched her wrist. Fen quickly pulled her away to assess the damage.

She reassured him, "I'm fine. It's nothing at all."

Ennis seethed, "Try that again, and it will be more than a scratch. Can't you see that I don't want to hurt you? I don't want to hurt any fae. I only want to return the world to its natural order: fae in the Otherworld, humans in theirs. Why is that so difficult to accept?"

"Not on my ship." Logan kicked the hilt of his sword into the air and caught it with his hand. He took a fighter's stance.

"Your word is my command, Captain." Ennis lifted the chain from out of his collar and aimed the talisman at Sal.

"No!" Raz leapt in front of him.

Beathan held her own talisman up to hit Ennis square in the chest with a blinding flash of white light.

The chain around Ennis's hand broke, and the talisman flew from his hands. Beathan's magic thrust Ennis violently into a pile of his own fae army. They all struck the wall with a thud. Ennis's force of energy, though broken, had not dissipated quickly enough. It hit Raz's shoulder, and he fell to the floor.

Sal caught him and turned him over. Carissa and Cameron ran to his side. Carissa touched his cheek, which was still warm, and Cameron checked for a pulse.

Somewhere over their heads, Carissa could hear Logan shouting orders and fae scrambling about, but her attention lingered on Raz. She searched around his neck and pulled up the chain. The talisman she'd given him was charred, burned up by Ennis's magic.

"The amulet the washer woman gave you—you gave it to Raz?" Cameron asked.

"I thought he might need protection if our spy found out he had the Talisman of Tethra. The washer woman said it would save someone who needed it the most."

"She also said that the talisman Ennis had would kill someone who was like family," Cameron said.

Neal bent and picked something up. Bringing it over to Carissa, he said, "It looks like the Talisman of Tethra was not damaged." He laid it in her hands.

"A dolphin tail? That's what all this fuss is about?" Tabitha asked.

Beathan brought the chain from off her neck and held it in front of a certain transforming crow. Raven, now human again, took the talisman. It was a conch shell with a glowing pearl. Raven recognized it immediately.

"Ennis's was a water fae talisman. This is the real Talisman of Tethra."

Carissa explained, "I switched the talismans. It was Raz's idea after we heard Neal fighting off an intruder near Raz's home when I visited him. We thought perhaps the spy knew Raz had the talisman and would try to steal it. When I knew Beathan wasn't the spy, I gave her the Talisman of Tethra."

"I knew then that you had taken a great leap of faith in trusting me, which is why I vouched for you in Hy Brasil. I'm only sorry I failed to protect your friend."

Logan rejoined them. "Ennis is gone. I'm uncertain whether he survived, but his fae have taken him and left the ship. We were only able to take a handful of prisoners. The rest may yet cause us trouble." He knelt alongside Carissa and Cameron and hung his head low. "Your friend was a hero. We'll take his body back to the Deep Rhys and see that he is laid to rest with honor."

"No, he's not—" Cameron began.

Raz's body jumped up suddenly, taking in ragged breaths.

Tabitha squealed and wrapped her magic around him. His body twisted against the restraint. He coughed.

"He's not dead!" Cameron said more forcefully this time.

"Tabitha! For goodness sakes, let him go!" Hela cried out.

"Sorry!" Tabitha's magic uncurled.

Raz breathed in deeply. "Let me say, Captain," he said between breaths, "first aid on your ship is seriously lacking."

Laughter rang out across the room. They helped Raz to his feet and examined the destruction on deck. The druids were already at work, turning the tables and chairs upright, repairing walls and rethatching the ceiling with their wands in hand.

"Don't worry. The *Scuabtuinne* has seen many a battle and always come out all the stronger for it."

Raven said, "Let's hope the same proves true for Moss Hill."

Chapter 20

Water Under the Bridge

Moss Hill needed some repair. Though the buildings might have been worse for the wear, the people were filled with hope. The people who were awake, that is. When they arrived, the passengers of the *Scuabtuinne* were greeted with the sight of sleeping citizens. There was also a handful of water fae walking around.

The first one they spotted, Chaos shot at with her faerie dust. The fae sneezed, then swayed, and eventually fell to sleep like the others. Cameron helped him make the trip to the ground without hurting himself.

"Chaos! These are seelie faeries. They're from the water city and here to help," Carissa chided.

Chaos put her hands up in the air and shrugged innocently. Hiya and Cynth helped revive the man with a few slaps of faerie dust to the face. Carissa did not envy him. A few seconds in, the fae awoke. Cameron helped him up.

"Sorry about the faeries. They get a little carried away," he said.

With a hand rubbing his jaw, the fae said, "No problem."

"How far along are you in capturing the unseelie?" Logan asked.

The fae bowed in recognition of Logan. "We've arrested a dozen so far. They've been taken to our prisons. We've woken some of the citizens we've identified as seelie. Macara has been helpful in that regard."

"How's Vale? Were there any unseelie there?" Hela asked.

The water fae shook his head. "I don't know. I've been assigned on patrol of this area only."

"Tabitha, you and I will pop over to Vale, shall we?" Raven said.

Tabitha nodded. "There's a portal on First Street. We can take that."

"Fen and I are coming, too! We must see how Father and Mother are doing." Hela and Fen walked briskly to catch up with the others.

"And me," Sal raised a hand before hastening to join them.

As they walked down the street, it became more and more obvious that the water fae were waking the citizens one by one, separating out the unseelie from the Mossie residents.

"Any particular place we should start?" Logan asked.

"City hall. We should see how Reg is doing," Cameron said.

Carissa nodded. "You go ahead and help the druids separate who's who. I'll go up to the Everly's. We may need Jane's help. Raz, you may want to join me."

Raz and Carissa diverged from the group to the long road up Aisling Mountain. When they arrived at the Everly mansion, Raz took off his hat and held it to his chest.

"My word," he said.

"Yes, they're the richest family in Moss Hill. Fudge is their butler." Carissa's eyes slid to gauge Raz's reaction.

Carissa interpreted his silence as nervousness, confirmed by the fact that he fidgeted with his hat. His exclamation of "oh no!" was unexpected. Carissa followed his eyes to the steps of the mansion.

Varick lay face-first on the pavement. Carissa ran to him and pressed her fingers against his neck.

"He's fine. He's just asleep."

"Are you sure he's not unseelie?" Raz asked.

"Varick is the captain of the sidhe guard in Moss Hill. He was probably coming here to see Jane."

"Is she the druidess of which you spoke earlier?"

Carissa nodded. "The most powerful in Moss Hill."

The door opened, and a woman's voice pitched in, "Which is precisely why Macara has already awoken Jane."

Carissa's eyes rested on the short bean tighe in a fall leaf-patterned dress. "Holly? Are you all right?"

The bean tighe walked down the steps of the home. "I'm fine, but Macara's having a day like no other. She was in Vale when everything went topsy-turvy. Cari, you should've seen it. I heard the sirens and the shouting all the way at the top of the hill. Closing the cottage windows didn't help, so I came down here to see what the fuss was and suddenly I'm lying in the hallway not three feet from Fudge. I heard him call out my name and then nothing."

"Where is he?" Raz stepped forward and tried looking through the open door behind Holly.

Her eyebrows knitted together. "He's asleep right where he dropped. Cari, who is this snoopy man?"

"Introductions later. Where is Macara?"

"She woke Jane and me and then took her straight away to Vale to wake the guard. I think she missed Varick there." Holly craned her neck to see past Carissa and Raz. Has he been there this whole time?"

Carissa bent and waved a hand over Varick's head. She allowed the Tuatha de Danann magic to flow through her. He stirred.

"Mmm, what happened?" Varick put a hand to his forehead.

"We should be asking you that," Carissa said.

She reached a hand out. He took it, rising to his feet. When he'd regained his senses, he tensed.

"The unseelie. They've infiltrated Moss Hill. It's worse than the changeling invasion. They're everywhere."

"I know that much. But where did they come from?"

"Some were posing as tourists; others came in on a ship today. They just started going mad all at once: starting fights, using their magic on citizens, and trying to turn Mossies and Vale residents against each other. We tried to calm them, but when we wouldn't turn against each other, they turned on us. That's when we realized they were unseelie."

Raz went inside to wake Fudge. Carissa saw him sitting up from the corner of her eye.

"Holly, stay here with Fudge. Raz, you stay, too. Holly makes a fine tea. It'll help after your near-death experience."

"Near-death?" Fudge shook his head as if struggling to process the information.

Carissa turned her attention back to Varick. "Come on. We have a town to protect."

***

WHEN ALL WAS said and done, they returned to the ship to retrieve their belongings. Rather than staying overnight, Logan decided to leave with the water fae. They had roughly fifty unseelie invaders to take to Tir-Na-Nog for trial.

Logan shook hands with Carissa. "We'll leave this island in your hands now, as it should be." He saluted Cameron. "You've proved yourself a worthy swordsman. There's always room on the *Scuabtuinne* for you, should you wish to join my crew."

Cameron smiled, saluting back. "Thank you, Captain, but my home is here in Moss Hill."

A sadness reached Logan's eyes as he smiled and walked down the dock.

"Logan," Carissa called him back. He turned. "I know the high seas are your life, but if you ever tire of traveling, I hope you'll consider Moss Hill your home, too."

Logan grinned. "I will."

Then he made his long strides up the gangway and disappeared over the rail. Cameron held an arm around Carissa. Tabitha watched them with watery eyes, shining in the reflected light of the morning sun. The twenty-four hours of the Tuatha de Danann's spell was over, and the mist around the island was gone. But a cloud still hung over their friend.

As they walked, Cameron and Carissa parted just enough to envelop Tabitha's shoulders between their arms. She walked with them to shore, clutching Otto's urn and fighting tears the whole way.

Ennis's defeat meant that order and balance were restored in Moss Hill, but he had taken a good man with him. Carissa wanted to think that Otto could survive the trip to the world beyond in spirit form.

"He's really gone, isn't he?" Tabitha cried.

Carissa squeezed her shoulders, saying, "Not as long as we remember him."

Tabitha's grip on the urn tightened. She sniffed and held the handkerchief to her face.

Carissa rubbed her back gently. "I'm so sorry, Tabitha."

Tabitha's breath hitched. "Otto had no soul, but he was his own person. He was alive, wasn't he?"

"Of course he was," Cameron assured.

"He, he couldn't have children, but he wanted them." Tabitha laughed. "We thought about taking in a changeling or crafting one ourselves from clay."

"You still can." Cameron shrugged. "I mean, anything's possible, isn't it?"

"Then, it's not crazy? I mean, it won't be him if I bring this clay back to life with changeling magic, but the clay will remember something of his personality. With his clay and my magic, it would be a child of ours."

Carissa wrapped an arm around her while trying to wrap her mind around the idea. That was how crimble changelings were made. It was how Otto had been brought to life. The idea seemed so strange. But then, Tabitha was strange. So maybe the idea fit her well.

"I can't tell you what to do. I can only say that whatever you choose, you'll have my support."

Tabitha wiped her eyes. It was a good thing, too, since Hela was disembarking at that very moment and would only be upset by the sight of tears. With her luggage in her husband's hands, and in the hands of five crewmen following her, Hela was free to rush to Tabitha's side.

"Is that Otto's urn? Oh, Tabitha, you dear, unfortunate girl. I can't even imagine what you're going through." She put her own arms around Tabitha, stealing her from Carissa's embrace. "There, there, we'll give him the best funeral Vale has ever seen."

Carissa smiled halfheartedly, knowing how few funerals a faerie village ever did see. Perhaps it was the thoughts of death and faeries that made her look far out to a secluded spot on the beach, where she spied a grim figure standing by the shore.

"I'll see you all later. You too, Cameron." She kissed him on the cheek.

"Where are you going?" Cameron asked.

Carissa replied just low enough for him to hear, "To see if a soul has made it into the world beyond."

Chapter 21

The World Is an Oyster

Alden agreed to meet Carissa the morning after Otto's funeral. She brought Tabitha to a prime spot on the coast to watch the sunrise. Alden appeared before them, his sight spooking Tabitha before he transformed back to his human guise.

"Did you bring me here just to give me a fright?"

"Actually, we're here to give you a gift. You were so distraught wondering whether Otto has a soul, and you were wondering about bringing a changeling child to life. We thought there was someone who might be able to answer both questions," Carissa explained.

Alden stepped aside. There was Otto in the same suit he'd passed away in, standing incorporeally on the rocky shore. Tabitha gasped. Forgetting herself, she tried to hug him. Her arms went right through.

"Careful now. I'm only a spirit," he said.

"But how?" Tabitha asked through tears.

"Our reaper friend allowed me to come back just long enough to say goodbye."

Carissa looked at Alden, tugging her head back to say that they should give the two some privacy.

"They'll have something important to discuss," Carissa said.

"I think we have something just as critical to talk about," Alden replied.

Carissa's eyebrow raised. "Oh? Didn't you tell me everything that happened here when we met the day we returned?"

"Yes. But you didn't tell me everything."

"What do you mean?"

"Carissa, I know that Raven gave the Talisman of Tethra to you."

"Just to keep safe. I don't intend to use it."

"Cameron told me what the washer woman said, that the talisman would cause someone who was family to die."

"But you said Niall was in the world beyond. Niall was my family, technically speaking. That means the prophecy was fulfilled."

Alden took her hand gently but firmly, saying, "Cari, he was talking to Cameron when he said that. Someone who was family to Cameron will die. The washer woman's prophecies are never wrong."

Carissa shook her head. "No. No, in a few more months, I'll be Cameron's family. Don't you see? That means by extension Niall was Cameron's family. It still works."

Alden thought for a moment and then let go. "I hope you're right, or just having it may put more people at risk."

"We won, Alden. Everything from here on out is going to be fine."

***

BY THE TIME Carissa said goodbye to Alden and parted ways with Tabitha at the portal on First Street, she heard a car honking. Cameron's car stopped right in front of Carissa. He rolled down the window. Still wearing his black suit from the funeral, Cameron looked at her with more mirth in his eyes than she expected.

"You disappeared after the funeral," Cameron said.

"Sorry, Tabitha insisted we take a portal to travel across town quickly. I'd have traveled back with her, but she insisted."

"Never mind that, I'm here. Get in. I want to show you something," Cameron said.

Carissa opened the door and scooted in.

"What is it?"

"If I told you, it wouldn't be a surprise." He held Carissa's hand as he drove up the hillside.

They passed city hall, the Seelie Tree Apothecary shop, and turned onto Greenfield, the road leading to Crescent Circle neighborhood.

"You're taking me back to my house?"

"You could say that," Cameron replied.

Surprisingly, he turned onto the road from Greenfield toward Vale Mountain.

"Where are we," Carissa started to ask, but seeing Cameron's lips pressed tightly into a grin told her he wasn't speaking and that he was ecstatic about his surprise.

Carissa smiled like Cameron's joy was contagious. They came to the base of the Village of Vale, and Cameron parked the car. Carissa was sure she had figured it out this time.

"My parents have a party planned at their house, don't they?" she asked.

Cameron's only response was to walk around the car, open Carissa's door, and extend a hand. He and Carissa walked up the steps to Vale. At the fork in the road, they turned toward Carissa's parents' cabin. Carissa took a step forward, but Cameron pulled her in a different direction.

Carissa's heart fluttered between confusion and joy as he opened the gate to their backyard. The gate was magically sealed, so the only way Cameron could have opened it was with her parents putting an enchantment on the talisman that served as Cameron's ring.

A gasp escaped Carissa's lips as she saw the whole garden lit with faerie lights and a changeling portal near the entrance.

Carissa turned to Cameron with an upraised eyebrow. A movement behind the portal caught Carissa's eye.

Tabitha emerged. "Sorry! I tried hiding. I'm not here. You didn't see me."

She tiptoed indoors.

"Why is Tabitha—"

Cameron held a finger to her lips. "Just wait."

Hand in hand, they stepped through the portal. They emerged on the other side to a breathtaking view. Carissa felt the world was swirling around her as she turned to take the whole sight in. The shore on one side, the lights of Vale and Moss Hill on the other, Carissa could see the whole island.

"We're on the top of Vale Mountain," Carissa surmised.

Finally, Cameron nodded. He walked to a wooden sign on the base of a mound.   Carved into the wood were the words: *Welcome to the Shae-Larke home.*

Carissa cocked her head questioningly.

Cameron explained, "The council gifted this land to us. Tabitha installed portals all over the island that we can access through this one, so you can be right in the Seelie Tree or at Nan's, or Macara's, or anywhere you want within minutes. Fenigar has agreed to design the architecture and oversee the human and fae builders who are going to create our perfect home. It'll be ready in time for our wedding. It is everything you told me you wanted...if I understood you right."

It took a moment for Carissa to speak. "You understand me perfectly. But is it what you want? I mean, you were still deciding what you wanted to do with your life. What if you want to travel? I don't think I want to be here alone."

"Sure, I want to travel on vacations with you. Carissa, I'm not going to be an ambassador, mayor of Moss Hill, or a member of the fae council.

"I'm glad that I was offered all those positions. It showed me that people have faith in me and what I can accomplish. But I can't just keep taking the opportunities that come to me.

It's time I show the same faith in myself and carve my own path with a vision of my own.

"This area isn't for the two of us. I just negotiated the details with Reg, but this is the site of a summer camp for human and fae children from all over the world to learn everything about the two worlds, about each other, magic and technology and every possibility that a future of unity has to offer. What do you think?"

Carissa's arms encircled Cameron's waist. "I think I'm marrying the best person I've ever met, human or fae."

They kissed under the moonlight on the top of the fae mountain overlooking their home.

"Now, you were right about the party at your parents', so we should probably get back there," Cameron said.

Carissa smiled. "I wouldn't miss it for the world."

Want more great content?

Hi, I'm Astoria Wright, the author of The Faerie Apothecary Cozy Mysteries. I hope you've enjoyed the first book in this series.

Check out the rest of
The Faerie Apothecary Mysteries:

Chaos in the Countryside
Herbs and Homicide
Remedy and Ruins
Elixirs and Elves
Charms and Changelings
Potions and Panic
Talismans and Turmoil
Tonics and Turning Points (Out December 2019)

To keep up with this series and others by the author, check out the website:

www.astoriawright.com

Sign up for the mailing list for updates and freebies available only to members!

A Note from Chaos:

Do you like this book?
I hope you do.
Please do me a favor
and leave a review!

Thanks for reading!

www.ingramcontent.com/pod-product-compliance
Lightning Source LLC
Chambersburg PA
CBHW022105170626
46808CB00002B/608